Dog Aliens 1
Raffle's Name

CHERISE KELLEY

Michele,
Thanks for your nice
review at amazon.com!

Cherie Kelley

DEDICATION

To everyone who has adopted a pet from the pound:
Bless you.

CONTENTS

GLOSSARY OF TERMS

Jex - Resource that the Kaxians and Niques mine here on Earth, the reason they are here, used for their bio-regenerating technology, which is how they have numerous lives, not a resource that is known by humans nor used by humans

Kaxians - Space aliens from the planet Kax, called "big dogs" by humans

Kanx - Kaxians' secret code for when they don't want the Niques to understand them

Niques - Space aliens from the planet Nique, called "little dogs" by humans

CHAPTER 1: JEX

"Come on, Mom, Dad! The humans won't be home for hours. Come mine with us! It's fun!"

"Your mother's mining days are over, Son, and so are your dad's. We know it's fun hanging out with your buddies, but other things come first for us now. You'll understand some day."

I nodded at them, but I doubted I would ever understand. My puppy self doubted anything could come first over having fun. The memories told me my Kaxian duty to mine must come first. I ran past all my holes that the humans had filled in, dug a new one, scrambled under the backyard fence, and skedaddled off to join my pack.

I checked the usual places for scent messages telling me where the day's dig was. I left my own scent message to let the rest of the pack know I would be there, too. So far, I could tell there were 12 of us already today.

Before too long, I made my way to the edge of civilization. We live in a suburb way east of Los Angeles, where civilization ends abruptly at the edge of a cactus and tumbleweed desert that stretches through mountains all the way to Las Vegas.

Our pack's mining tunnel was about four Kaxians wide and ten Kaxians long. It went into the side of a hill, so it didn't slant down too much. The pack was gathered at the mouth of the tunnel, which faced away from civilization, toward the open desert.

"Clem! Over here!"

Clem is my Kaxian name, so I answered.

"Hi guys!"

Eight of the twelve of us present today were puppies, under a year old, like me. I ran over and joined two of my fellow puppies: Lido and Skil.

Lido is mostly an English bulldog this life, a little older than me, seven months to my six. Don't tell him I said this, but Lido's humans feed him a little too much. Well, a lot too much. My best friend Lido is portly, OK? I mean, I know bulldogs are heavyset to begin with. It's not that. We're talking his belly almost touches the ground. He's a good friend, though.

Skil is a female black Labrador retriever this life, and a little younger than me at five months. She's easygoing, one of those dogs who always rolls onto her back when she meets a new human, in hopes that the human will rub her belly. We Kaxians call her type a 'pet-me.' She pretty much goes along with whatever Lido and I want to do, so long as she gets her turn.

The pack was getting ready for the mining strategy meeting. Lately, I had noticed a pattern at these meetings. To test my theory, I sat down a little away from Skil, the whole time making eye contact with Lido. Sure enough, Lido turned to face Skil and sat next to her. Us guys used to always stick together, so I didn't know what was up with that, but it'd been going on for a week or so.

Koog, one of the pack's mining leaders, coughed to get our attention.

Lido was staring all gooey eyed at Skil, so I kicked some dirt at him. He looked up at me, mad.

"Hey! What the..."

Everyone else was looking at him, and the rest of the puppies laughed.

Koog raised his eyebrow at Lido.

Lido looked down at the ground and kicked some dirt to the side.

"Sorry."

Koog cleared his throat, scowled playfully at Lido, and went over the day's mining assignments. First, he addressed the two adult miners who were present today.

"Crash and Trixie will be our main diggers."

They both raised their chins at Koog, to show they had heard his orders.

"Clem, Lido, and Skil, you three pull the dirt out of the front of the tunnel, after Crash and Trixie dig it up, so that the tunnel stays clear all the way through and the diggers don't bury themselves. After a while, we will switch so that you three get your turns on the jex, too."

We tried to raise our chins to Koog in acknowledgment, as Crash and Trixie had, but Koog slanted his head to the side, so we were forced to speak.

"Yes, Sir."

Crash and Trixie flexed their muscles while still laying back, looking cool.

Koog continued his instructions. We listened carefully, even though we had heard them several times before. We were puppies, which meant we

3

could be disciplined for not listening.

"Everyone, while we are mining, be sure to listen for any warnings from Heg's defense team. If you hear a warning, go to the opening of the tunnel where we will all meet to help defend it. Let's go mine!"

Lido, Skil, and I worked out a rotation where we each took a turn getting dirt thrown on us while we picked it up from where the other three miners threw it. Our other turns were spent picking up the dirt from where the one it landed on threw it. That's how it was supposed to work, anyway. It looked to me like Lido was taking all of Skil's turns at the part where he got dirt thrown on him.

There was dirt flying everywhere: paws throwing dirt and coats shaking off more dirt. It was fun!

Koog, Crash, and Trixie were taking turns with one digging the vein of jex and the other two digging away the sides from where the main jex miner dug, so that the main digging channel wouldn't cave in.

The dirt was piling up faster than I could clear it away.

"I need some help here!"

Koog sized up the situation.

"Crash, Trixie, help Clem and them!"

Crash helped me clear, and Trixie helped Skil and Lido move the dirt farther away, outside our tunnel. The two of them were adult Kaxians already, a few years old. The puppy in me felt proud to be working with them, side by side, as equals.

I felt even happier when I took my turn digging into the vein of jex. It was a big vein, enough to keep us busy for another month. If all of us showed up every day, we could beat our quota. That would look good on my record, and might help me get a promotion, once I was no longer a puppy. Being a miner is fun, but being on the defense team and looking out for the Niques seems like it would be even more fun. Even better, leading mining or guarding operations gets you more respect.

As fast as I dug up the jex, I ingested it. I could carry quite a bit this way, and only other "dogs" would notice how loaded down and slow-moving I was. I would excrete it later, ten miles away, so that the crew could load it onto the nearest Kaxian space shuttle and take it to one of our star ships.

I was all loaded up on jex and ready to head for the shuttle and make my delivery when the Niques showed up, of course.

One of our six lookouts, a yellow Great Dane puppy named Lis, spotted them and yelled out the dreaded warning.

"Niques!"

The Niques were the reason we had the mining meetings. They were why we took our procedures so seriously. We didn't want the Niques stealing our jex! As we had pre-arranged, we all met with our faces sticking out of the tunnel, clogging it up with our rear ends to block the Niques from gaining entrance to the jex mine. This was tough because they were all so little they could fit under our bellies.

"Clem, put your legs behind mine!"

"Lis! There's a gap over here!"

As was their style, the Niques taunted us from just outside the tunnel:

"We'll make you move!"

"You can't stay there all day!"

"Give it up, Kaxians."

"There's plenty of jex for all of us."

The Niques employed their usual strategy of making so much noise that sooner or later a human would come over and either chase us away or catch us and take us to the pound.

Heg, our defense leader, kept us moving toward our goal.

"Lido, you go to the space shuttle first."

I thought that made sense. If Lido's, um, girth gave him any trouble it was best he went first. That way, the rest of us would be along soon to help him.

"All right. Hope to see you soon."

Now that the Niques were here, we all spoke in code, of course. Our ordinary speech sounds a lot like the barking of wolves, which is why Kax chose Earth. You already had a species which is very similar to Kaxians, so similar that hardly any of us are full Kaxians anymore. The Niques' ordinary speech was always similar enough that they understood ours. That's why we use a code called Kanx: when we don't want the Niques to understand us. (The Niques have their own code they use when they don't want us to understand, too, but who cares about them?)

Lido took off running as fast as he could, and the rest of us pressed tightly into the opening he left.

Three of the fastest Niques in their pack took off after Lido. They were so little that it would take three of them to carry all the jex he was carrying, if they managed to trap him so that he couldn't make it to the shuttle before his jex came out.

As my parents had taught me, I said a silent

prayer to Kax. I prayed that Lido would outrun those three "little dogs." I asked that Kax help the rest of us stay long enough to block the ten "little dogs" that remained, and that something would draw the "little dogs" away so that the rest of us could make it to the shuttle. And, I asked Kax to please find a way to see that I would get my promotion. I know, I know. That last part was selfish of me, but that was what I prayed. At least I was honest and said so!

The Niques were up to their annoying little schemes, as usual.

"Humans, come chase these selfish Kaxians away from this tunnel!"

"Yeah, they are selfish!"

"They always try and keep all the jex for themselves!"

If the Niques would've just shut up, this wouldn't have been stressful at all. The biggest Nique here was a Shih Tzu, and most of them were much smaller: a Pekingese, a Tibetan Terrier, a Lhasa Apso, three Maltese, and a chihuahua. (This is Southern California; there's always a chihuahua.) The Niques didn't stand a chance fighting us, but they were smart enough to know it.

Humans often think a little dog (Nique) is trying to pick a fight with a big dog (Kaxian). In actual fact, the Niques always just try to annoy us Kaxians enough so we will get in trouble with the humans and get sent to the pound. Annoying Kaxians is what the Niques do. It's their purpose in life. Well, that, and stealing our jex.

Half to annoy us, and half to make trouble for us with the humans, the Niques started shouting out lies in the wolf language that everyone but the humans understood:

"Humans!"

"Come help us, humans!"

"These big dogs are going to hurt us!"

Three humans were walking down the sidewalk on the edge of civilization. They were all young males: past puberty, but not by much.

"Great," I thought, "school must be out for the day. It's getting late. My human will be home soon, and I need to be in the yard, or he will find the hole I dug under the fence."

Our defense leader, Heg, once again kept us focused on the task at hand.

"Turn around and look like you're hunting something inside the tunnel."

Oddly, when Heg said that, I thought I saw a picture of all of us looking like wolves and hunting some prey that was digging into the tunnel. It must have been my imagination, but it was pretty vivid, and showed me exactly where to fit into the tunnel mouth between Skil and Crash. The Niques were in the picture, too, only they also looked like wolves, baby wolves who were also hunting the prey that was tunneling. The picture flashed in my mind for only a second, and then it was gone.

I decided to think about the picture later, to figure out what it meant and why I had seen it. Right now, I was in a big hurry to get to this empty spot I noticed, between Skil and Crash. I thought it would be a good spot for me to add to the blockade and help prevent the Niques from getting into our mine.

All of us Kaxians turned around so that our faces were inside the hole. We scrambled, dug, and kept talking. so that we would resemble wolves hunting. But, we kept the Niques out of our mine.

The Niques bit our rear ends, in an attempt to get us annoyed enough to make mistakes.

We kicked the Niques and dug up dirt into their eyes.

Then, they actually helped us look like a pack of wolves hunting prey in a tunnel by talking a lot, themselves, although if the humans knew what they were saying, they wouldn't think the Niques were so cute anymore.

"Oh that's right, show us your pretty side."

"No! Turn around and fight us!"

"You cowards!"

Heg's plan worked. The three young male humans just kept on walking by. They must have thought we were all one big pack of dogs, hunting together for prey that was tunneling.

We were still stuck guarding our jex from the Niques instead of taking it to the shuttle, though.

I spoke to Heg in Kanx.

"Want me to lead three more Niques away?"

"Yeah, good idea. Go!"

As fast as I could, I took off running toward the nearest Kaxian space shuttle, up in the foothills nearby, about a ten-mile jog. Sure enough, three Niques followed me.

I was running fast, and it wasn't even difficult, even though I was loaded down with jex. I ran like the wind and jumped from boulder to boulder, leaving my Nique pursuers far behind. I had finished dumping my load by the space shuttle before I even heard the three Niques again.

The Kaxian in me had always appreciated these long legs I have, this life. I get them from my mom, who's a Queensland Heeler from Australia. Dad's a German Shepherd, mostly, and his legs aren't short, but Mom wins every time they race. The shuttle crew had ingested my load and I was free to run off before the Niques even caught up to me.

That's when I saw Lido. He still had a long way to make it up the hill. He was gasping for breath, and his three Niques were nipping at his tail.

I wasn't sure what I was going to do to help Lido, but he was my pack mate. I knew I had to help him. I went bounding down the side of the hill he was climbing. As I jumped from place to place as fast as I could, I said the quickest prayer to Kax ever:

"Help!"

I didn't hear any answer. I did get lucky, though. On one of my jumps, I unexpectedly landed in a pile of stones. They loosened and all started tumbling down the hill toward Lido and the Niques.

Lido's big belly just barely cleared the stones, but he jumped over them.

The Niques were too small to jump over the stones. They turned around and ran down the hill! They ran fast enough to not get killed, but slow enough that they wouldn't be coming after us for a few days. I took great satisfaction in seeing them turn their tails and run away.

My three Niques had just crested the hill. They now stood in the way of Lido reaching the space shuttle and unloading his jex. Thank Kax, we were next to a particularly steep part of the hill, which hid us from their view. It didn't hide us from their noses, but we would just have to gamble they didn't catch on. I had a plan.

"Give me your jex."

Lido found a suitably clean place without thorns, spun to mash the tall wild grasses down, and dumped his load of jex.

I ingested it.

"We'll run down the hill where they can see us, Lido, and then you go right and I'll go left. So far as they know, you have the jex. Hopefully, they'll think you're taking it to the next shuttle, and they'll all follow you. Then, I can take the jex to this shuttle."

"OK!"

We took off running down the hill. Well, I took off. Lido kind of lumbered off, but he was doing the best he could. Don't laugh!

The Niques followed as soon as they saw us. Sure enough, when we split up, they all three followed Lido. He was just headed home, but they wouldn't know that until he passed by the trail up to the next Kaxian space shuttle.

I moseyed on up to our nearby space shuttle and dropped my second load of jex for the day, smiling the whole time. Looking out for my friend, I followed Lido's scent until I was sure he had made it safely home, and then I headed home, myself.

***

Scrabbling under my back-yard fence, I heard my human coming home in his car.

"Whew!" I thought, "Made it home just in time."

I was so busy being pleased with myself for outsmarting those Niques that I didn't notice the fresh footprints next to my hole under the fence, or the fresh human scent that should have told me my parents' human had already been home today.

11

CHAPTER 2: THE SIDES

As the Kaxians see things:

When we left Kax, almost 1,000 dog-lives ago, our mission was to come here to Earth, set up jex mining and shipping teams, and then work them in shifts. Each Kaxian was only supposed to remain on Earth for 5 lives and then go back home with the next shipment.

It hasn't worked out that way.

We never counted on the Niques following us and trying to steal our jex.

Now, we are stuck in a constant battle with them to keep even half the jex that gets mined on Earth. We spend more energy and effort defending what should be ours than we spend mining it, all because the greedy little Niques won't honor our prior claim to the mining rights.

I say 'battle,' but you humans would hardly recognize it as such. Your technology runs toward weaponry. Ours runs toward biology.

We rebirth into limitless lifespans, with some restrictions. Tweaking that process consumes almost all of our intellectual energy, so that not much at all is left for weaponry. The process makes some of us especially vulnerable to bonding with humans, so even if we had weaponry, we couldn't use it against humans. Not now. Maybe in the beginning we could have, but that was long ago.

You humans don't even use jex, so you don't miss it. We are not a threat to you.

This was supposed to be a mining and shipping operation, albeit a covert one. We had neither planned nor provisioned for a knock-down, drag-out fight lasting almost 1,000 dog lives.

No one has been allowed to go home to Kax.

Many have died and not been reborn.

More of us have had to come from Kax to help in the defense efforts.

We chose Earth because you already had wolves, animals that closely resembled us, and so we were able to easily fit in and assimilate into your Earth society. You had started to domesticate some of your native wolves, so it was only natural that you would also "domesticate" us, animals that resembled wolves.

Yes, we can breed with wolves, so most "dogs" are not fully aliens. Only a handful remain who came on the original mission from Kax. Perhaps a dozen full Kaxians who came on later ships remain.

The rest of us were born here on Earth and have never seen our home world. We Earthborn still think of ourselves as Kaxians, but many of us genuinely love humans. It is not that way with those few who came on ships from Kax and who remember our world.

***

As the Niques See Things:

There is plenty of jex here for everyone. The Kaxians are just greedy bullies. We were scouting Planet Earth at the same time as the Kaxians, so we contest their claim. So what if they landed first? So what if they discovered the first jex vein, and started mining first?

We provided the urinary-tract message system technology, which they gladly adopted without so much as a "Thank you." This technology is part of what has allowed us all to operate covertly on Earth for close to 1,000 dog lives now. We feel that sharing this technology with the Kaxians entitles us to an equal share of the jex.

Besides, they dare not attack us en masse. That would spoil the illusion that we are all "domesticated" animals, subservient to humans. Neither of us has defense technology sufficient to withstand the superior size or strength of the people of Earth. It has always been so.

Nique and Kaxian technology runs toward bio-regenics. Long before either of us came to Earth, both our societies made it possible to transfer our consciousness from one body to the next. This is such an advantageous line of research that we spend all our resources on it. Weapons are just not something we do, in either of our cultures.

We prefer it this way: we infiltrate other worlds, pose as pets, and quietly mine and ship our jex behind the scenes. You humans don't use jex, so we are not a threat to you. (The Kaxians aren't, either, but who cares about them?)

We Niques are smaller than the Kaxians, so we fit into smaller tunnels. We mine where they can't. They just feel superior because they are larger. The Kaxians have no more of a legitimate claim on Earth or on the humans than we Niques have.

And anyway, the humans love us "little dogs" more.   We're   cuter.

CHAPTER 3: CAR TRIP

Wow, my parents' human was taking me somewhere in the car alone, just the two of us! This was the first time that had ever happened. I had been in the car before, to go to the dog park or to the vet, but Mom and Dad had always been along, and my brothers and sisters, before other humans had adopted them.

This was going to be a long car trip. I could tell because I smelled food in the bag he had thrown into the back seat. Maybe he would drive us to the woods and then take me for a long walk, and we would explore a wilderness area together! This was odd so late in the day, but hey, if we spent enough time alone together having fun, we might finally bond. I would like that. At least, I thought I would like that.

My previous life memories about the dog bond were a bit hazy. I could remember everything I ever knew about mining jex. I could remember several hundred commands that humans had taught me, in my previous lives. I knew that humans could bond with Kaxians (and with Niques, but who cared about them?). Everyone said the dog bond was lovely, something to strive for. I thought probably I had bonded with humans before, but I honestly could not remember for sure, and I could not remember what it was like. I thought it would be nice, though.

I looked over at this human who had bonded with my parents, to try and catch some body language that told me what he was thinking, where we were going, or anything interesting at all.

He didn't look at me, not even a glance ever, for the two hours we were in the car together.

I thought this was strange, but I made excuses for him. This was my first time riding in the front seat, and he was driving, after all. "Maybe he finds driving too engrossing a task, and can't take his attention away from driving to look at me. Yeah, that's probably it," I told myself.

He switched on the radio and sang along with some nonsensical songs, hitting the steering wheel to the beat of the music, and pretty much ignoring me. He answered his phone and chatted about his job with a female. He looked out the window as the sun set, whistling a tune.

I told myself, "Just be content that he took you along," and I did my best to look like I was having fun. I looked out the window, too, and watched the desert go by.

After ninety minutes or so, he turned, and we were going up a mountain road. My parents' human did drive up into the woods! It seems a long way to any woods, from the deserts of Southern California, but there are huge pine trees a few hours' drive away, up any of the local mountains.

It was dark when he stopped the car and set the parking brake, which again, I thought was odd. Humans don't see well in the dark. He put on a coat, put the small bag of food on his back, let me out, and called me to follow him over to where a trail headed off into the woods. How nice! We were going for a walk together!

I ran to him quickly, wagging my tail to show him how happy I was to be singled out and taken for a walk, all on our own. I wasn't even on a leash!

It was a lovely walk in the woods, even if it was a bit short. We went up a little hill. There were many different types of insects in the nearby bushes, chirping at us. I could smell lizards, snakes, squirrels, and gophers. There were no other humans around, which I figured was why I wasn't on a leash. The puppy that I was (and perhaps the wolf part of me) wanted to chase after a squirrel that ran across the trail. Memories from previous lives told me the human wanted me to stay by his left heel, though, so I did.

My parents' human sighed then. This confused me. I was 99% sure he wanted me to walk by his left heel and not chase the squirrel. I was doing what he wanted, so why was he unhappy?

We walked over the top of the little woodsy hill and down into a small valley where there were no trees, but grass grew so tall that I couldn't see over it. The trail wound on through the grass.

I could smell still water up ahead, which meant there was a lake, and I grew curious about what we would find there.

My parents' human stopped at the bottom of this little valley and took the bag off of his back.

So, I sat down nearby. I thought maybe he would pet me now, and talk to me. Maybe we would play that game where he chose a stick, had me sniff it, and then threw it and dared me to find it and bring it back to him. Perhaps we... Oh! Wow! Some of that food I could smell in his bag was for me!

He put some wonderful-smelling raw beef in a large bowl and set it down in front of me!

Incredulous, I looked at him for approval. He made the signal to eat! Unable to believe my good fortune, I set about chewing up all this luscious beef. It was quite chewy, and it took a bit of doing to eat, but it was delicious, far better than the dry dog food I was used to. Yum! I closed my eyes and relished every juicy bite.

In the back of my mind, I was aware that my parents' human was walking back up the hill, the way we had come. I could hear his footsteps. Oh! This meat was so good! Yum, yum! I munched contentedly.

When I heard the car start, I realized what was going on. He was going to leave me here! I had been caught digging my way out and leaving the yard over and over again these past few months. His scent had been there when I returned, and his footprints, but I hadn't consciously noticed. I was a fool, thinking I had gotten away with my disobedience. As a result, I was being abandoned.

I took off running, but even my fast legs didn't get me over that small hill before the car sped off, leaving me in the dust.

Fool that I was, I ran after the car, thinking maybe he was kidding, or maybe he would change his mind and stop to let me get in. I stayed with the car for almost a minute before it got going so fast down the mountain road that I couldn't keep up. I kept running after it at my full speed for thirty more minutes, and then I had to stop and rest. I plunked down right there at the side of the road, near the foot of the mountain, gasping for breath.

As the immediacy of running after the car faded and I caught up with my breathing, despair sank in. I had been abandoned by my parents' human. I was sure I could make my way back to his house tonight, but at the same time, I was equally certain the human there would not let me enter. Everything I would now do without came flooding into my mind for me to grieve over.

I had watched my parents race each other for the last time. I was sure Mom would always win, but it had been fun to watch and cheer her on. No more. There would be no more wrestling with Dad. He always won that, but I was growing. I had hoped that some day I would start to win, at least sometimes. Now, I would never know. I also wouldn't see my next batch of brothers and sisters born, or help raise them as Mom and I had planned together. I never even knew how nice I had it, until I lost it all.

I had been expunged, excommunicated, kicked out. The worst part was that in human terms I deserved it. My parents' human could never know about things like Kaxian duty. From his point of view, I was completely in the wrong. I had repeatedly dug holes under his fence, against his commands. No wonder he didn't want me. I didn't blame him. That just made me feel worse, not better. Being in the right was no consolation for feeling so alone and so unwanted.

Out of habit, I sniffed the air.

I smelled water down in the ravine that paralleled the mountain road. It smelled like it would soothe what ailed me, so I half ran, half slid down the hill to the creek that bubbled by. The water on the sides of the creek smelled off, but in the center it was clean. I waded in and drank my fill. The cool water did soothe my tired muscles, but now I was wet, and it wasn't that warm at night, up here in the woods, even though it was summer.

I sniffed the air again.

Kaxians had been here. There was hardly any place on Earth we hadn't been in the thousand dog lives since we first arrived on the planet. None of us had been here in at least a month, though. The scents were that old and faded. The scents were only minimally comforting. Sure, I could follow them and find others of my kind, but I didn't recognize the individuals who had left any of the Kaxian scents here. (I smelled some Nique scents, too, but who cares about them? Besides, they weren't recent enough to matter.)

My nose told me that this place was pretty isolated. Besides humans traveling on the road in vehicles, and a few wolves passing through on their hunting trips, nothing larger than a raccoon had been here in a week. Oh, there were a few fish in the creek. There were some beavers, squirrels, snakes, birds... OK, yes, there was plenty of food here. My parents' human had been at least considerate enough not to leave me in the stark desert where I might starve. I was still full from all that raw beef that had tricked me into getting abandoned here, though. What bothered me was there was no one for company, no one to talk to who would understand me.

For the briefest of seconds, I considered following the recent wolf scent. Wolves would understand me when I spoke. They had packs the same way as Kaxians, too. If I could find a wolf pack, I might have a new family. Wolf instinct told me that I could find the female who had passed by here not long ago. But would she accept me as one of her own kind? I was only the tiniest bit wolf. I was also only six months old.

A strange thing happened then.

A little movie played in my mind. In one way, it was like the Kaxian memories: it came to me in vivid moving pictures that I could also hear and smell. In another way, it was unlike the memories. That's just it: this was something new, not a memory. I had no idea where it came from.

In this mental movie, I was following the she-wolf's scent. I followed it for a day, down this mountain, across some wild desert, over some hills, and halfway up a different mountain.

I saw the she-wolf then, not twenty feet from me. She was alone between two large boulders, licking one of her paws. She was a bit older than me, about nine months old. She stopped mid-lick when she sensed me nearby. Our eyes met. Her scent came to me on the wind: female and sweet, but wild and untamed.

"Hello. I'm Clem."

"Hello. I'm Neya."

She put her paw down and stood up straight. Her eyes remained locked on mine while her nostrils flared a few times. She made a pretty picture, standing there.

I caught myself staring slack-jawed and stood up as straight as I could, hoping to pass muster.

She slowly walked toward me, sniffing. Her

tail was wagging slowly, and her ears were up, both giving away her intent to play with me.

I crouched down on my front legs, ready to pounce on her when she got to me, but being obvious about it, giving her plenty of warning that I planned to pounce on her. Playing.

She matched my pouncing posture.

We both wagged our tails quickly now, giving away that we were both having fun. Our eyes were still locked together, but that was fun, too.

She was close enough now that her scent intoxicated me. I imagined our future together: joining her pack and becoming her mate. I saw us running together through spring flowers, summer green grass, fall leaves, and winter snow. We slept side by side, at first alone, and then with a litter of pups born in a small cave near here.

I pounced on her, and we went rolling over each other, quickly nipping necks and ears but still wagging our tails in happy play. And then we both heard the rest of her pack yelling about an intruder, and our tails and ears went limp.

"Goodbye, Clem."

"Goodbye, Neya."

Neya's wolf pack ran after me, shouting out how I didn't belong with them, and how I had better run...

I shook off that strange spell that had come over me. Of course I couldn't follow the wolf scent.

What was I thinking? I wasn't thinking. I was just feeling. Feeling lonely enough to fantasize about a she-wolf!

I shook myself again.

I was so lonely that I wouldn't even mind

being annoyed by the Niques right now. The Niques were obnoxious, and they did try to get us Kaxians sent to the pound, but unlike the wolves, the Niques wouldn't eat me! At least, I was 99% sure they wouldn't. Not in town, anyway.

I howled in sorrow. My howl echoed off the mountains and came back to me, eerily as if I did have company.

But wait. Oh yeah! My parents had taught me that I was never alone. They had told me that if I ever felt lonely, all I had to do was pray to Kax and I would have all the company I needed. I was doubtful, but I was also out of options, so I tried it. I prayed to Kax.

"What will I do? Where will I go? Help! I'm all alone. Can you keep me company? Hello?"

I didn't hear any answer.

Coincidentally, right then my logical Kaxian memories took over and quenched the despair my puppy brain was feeling at being cut off from Mom and Dad. They had taught me that deep down inside me, my logical Kaxian self waited to be remembered, as I grew up. Now, logic told me that my pack could still use my help guarding the jex and mining, and that my Kaxian duty was to get to the mine as quickly as I could. The pack would find me a place to sleep and bring me food to eat.

Wow. I had a duty. I belonged to a pack! I already had a destination and a purpose. I already had twenty friends for company; I just had to get back to them. What was I doing wallowing around here in the muddy creek?

On my way back up to the road, I noticed that the logical, old-memory part of my brain was making calculations. I had been in the car with the human for just over two hours, and the car had been going an average of 68 miles per hour, so the valley where I had been abandoned was about 130 miles from my neighborhood, the old-memory part of my brain reckoned.

But, I had run full tilt back toward the neighborhood for half an hour before stopping here to rest and get some water. I have no idea how, but my Kaxian logic figured I had run at a rate of 24 miles per hour. So, I was about 118 miles from my neighborhood.

Furthermore, all by itself, without my input, energy, or initiative, my Kaxian memory figured I could reliably travel 15 miles per hour, with stops for rest, so it told me I would be back with the pack in just under 8 hours. My Kaxian memories also told me it wasn't safe to run on the highway, so I ran alongside it, toward home.

CHAPTER 4: RANDY

I was down the mountain now, running beside the flat two-lane highway that went out east to the desert that I called home. It was pitch black out. The moon and stars could not shine through the clouds and smog that covered the sky. The only light came when a car passed by, which was every few minutes, even way out here, in the middle of the night.

Another car whizzed by me.

I was tired, cold, and lonely, but determined to get back home to Lido, Skil, and the rest of my pack.

"Hm," I thought. "It would certainly be faster and easier to ride back to town in a car." The next time I heard one coming (from miles away, because I can hear pretty well), I was daydreaming how nice it would be if the driver stopped and opened the door to let me get in.

Almost reflexively, I found myself praying to Kax. Out of habit, whenever I get stressed out, I pray to Kax for help. My prayers are not the formal, "get on your knees" type. Nope. They happen more in the moment, mostly when I need help or when I have to make   a   decision.

This time, my prayer sounded like this:

"Could you get one of these drivers to give me a ride?"

I didn't hear any answer.

However, something gave me the idea to concentrate on the mind of the approaching driver and think about what I wanted to happen. Even more than that, I saw another mental movie, this time, of myself showing the driver a mental movie: the driver stopping the car in front of me and offering me a ride.

I shook myself.

What a weird idea!

"I must be over tired, to have all these visions coming at me."

I said it to no one in particular. Oh great. Now I was talking to myself. That's the first sign of insanity, right?

I had never heard of anything like this before. I was thinking, "Where in the world are these visions coming from? Am I a nut case now?"

But, then I thought, "What do I have to lose? If I die, I'll be reborn. It's not like I'm a helpless human. They really should be afraid of hitching rides."

All this happened in a few seconds. The car was still behind me. I still had time before it passed me by. But what was I supposed to do? How was I supposed to give the driver a vision?

Wait a sec.

"Kax! How do I give the driver a vision?"

I didn't hear any answer.

Following a sudden inspiration I had, I concentrated and closed my eyes. In my mind's eye, I searched for the driver's mind.

There it was!

With my eyes closed, it was as if I could actually see the driver's mind. It looked like a bundle of strings that I knew were thoughts and feelings, coming toward me at sixty miles per hour. It had a blueish color to it, which something told me meant the driver's mind was calm.

Focusing my inner eyes on the driver's mind, I made up a movie in my imagination, and I concentrated on showing my movie to the driver. My movie showed his car stopping a little ahead of where I ran. Don't ask me how, but just from the sound of it approaching, I knew to show his 2006 Chrysler 300C in my mental movie. It was so dark out I just left the color gray, figuring the color wouldn't be important, and then the car turned out to be a dark slate gray.

My suggestion took.

The driver slowed down, and then stopped.

I kept running until I got near his car, and then I stopped, out of his reach. Just because he stopped for me didn't mean he wouldn't hurt me.

I'm a Kaxian, so the rules are different for me than they are for humans, especially young humans. I tell you this because what happened next would almost certainly not happen for a human.

Concentrating on the driver's mind again, I showed him another mental movie. This time, I suggested that if he opened the passenger door, I would jump in, as if it were business as usual.

Making a funny face, the human walked around the car, opened the passenger door wide, and stepped back.

Sure enough, I jumped in, as if it were

business as usual and he had been letting me into his car my whole life. Which at six months was not very long, but you get the idea.

Well, I had a ride to town. How about that.

My belly was full. My bladder was empty. I had a few hours to kill, and it was warm in the car.

I fell fast asleep.

Yawn.

Blink. Blink.

When I woke up, it was because the driver was snapping a leash onto my collar.

Wait a minute, what?

"Come on, Dog. You can't sleep in the car. That's it. Come on upstairs." He gestured toward a stairwell in a white-stuccoed twenty-unit apartment building, which was in a complex with ten other such buildings. The place looked neat and smelled clean. It was quiet. All the lights were out, as it was still the middle of the night. And then he said something that decided it for me.

"Millie is going to love you!"

That sounded encouraging! And, as it happened, I did need a place to live. I could smell scents from my pack, distantly, but I definitely smelled them, which meant they would smell me and know where I was.

Yes, he did have a leash on me. He probably thought I had no choice. But, I chose to stay with him. I was looking forward to meeting Millie. She must be a human, because I didn't smell any recent non-human scents on him.

"You are one lucky dog, or maybe I am one lucky guy. I was planning on getting a dog, to please Millie. I already bought dog food, dog dishes, a leash, and a collar. I just got a free dog, and it looks like I can go get my money back for the collar. All in all, you cost me less than fifty bucks!"

"Happy to oblige," I told him.

Of course, all he heard when I spoke was the noise a wolf makes when it barks.

Still, I wanted to get along with my new human, so when he spoke to me, I looked at him and wagged my tail.

Before we got to the stairs, I got a vision of his apartment, and it did not have a doggie door like my parents' humans' home had.

Uh oh!

Think fast!

I played him a mental movie of walking me over to the nearby tree.

My suggestion took.

He complied, and I did my business.

We went up the stairs, and he opened his apartment door with his key. Sure enough, there was no doggie door. Good thing I had thought fast. Excited at being let inside his den, I paced the whole place in the first thirty seconds.

My new human's apartment was all beige inside: beige carpet, beige walls, beige doors, even beige furniture. There wasn't anything extra, like the bookshelves, buffet, wardrobes, and decorations my parents' humans had. There was a couch, a TV, a desk with a computer, a bed, and a dining room table. That was it. Everything smelled new. Well, except in the bathroom. And in the kitchen. The kitchen smelled much better than the bathroom!

There was no one else in the apartment, so while he changed into his pajamas, he spoke to me often. That suited me. I would just as soon know what was going on.

"I guess you'll be OK here in the apartment tomorrow while I'm at work."

"Sure, that suits me fine."

"I didn't get you a bed. You can lie down on the floor to sleep. Stay off the couch."

"OK."

"Millie is coming over tomorrow night for dinner. Ooh wee! She is going to love you!"

Once more, mention of a human who was going to love me made me glad I had decided to stay with my new human. I smelled her scent here. She had been in his den before, but only in the first room. She probably wasn't trusted well enough to be in the whole den, like I was. I would have to be a little cautious when she arrived.

I followed my new human into the kitchen and sat down to wait for him to talk to me some more. While I waited, I cleaned up some food spills on the kitchen floor. Mmmmm, this one was beef stew. Ooh! And this one here was ravioli! I found a few more places to clean up, on the cabinets as well as the floor, and for a while I didn't notice how quiet my new human had become.

However, once he had instructed me to stay off the couch, he proceeded to ignore me as he microwaved a frozen dinner, grabbed two beers out of the fridge, and vegged in front of the TV until he slumped off to bed.

I was still full from the beef I had been abandoned with, but it alarmed me just a tad that my new human hadn't offered me any of the dog food I could smell from where it was stashed in a closet.

Oh well. I was feeling a little smug in my new ability to suggest actions for humans to perform. I could always suggest that he feed me, and perhaps I would, in the morning.

For now, I had a roof over my head, and the carpeted floor looked far more comfortable than sleeping in the pack's mine. I was back in town.

***

Neya shook herself.

Disoriented, she looked around the cave where she had slept. It was the same cave she had just been dreaming about, but instead of her own pups and her (!) mate, there were her mother's pups, and her mother. Her father must be out hunting with the rest of the pack.

What an odd dream she just had! It seemed so real. And what kind of wolf had her dream mate been? Like no other she had ever seen before, that's what kind. His scent reminded her of the space aliens her parents had warned her about, those the humans called "dogs." Still, he'd been handsome.

He had given her his full attention, too, unlike the wolves in her pack, who were always half concentrating on prey or on human threats, or both. He had been play fighting with her, but unlike the touch of her litter-mates when they play fought, his touch had felt gentle, loving even.

How could she remember his touch if it was just a dream? It had to be more than a dream. He had been so real, so much fun, so attentive to her. They had hunted, nested. And they had been together so long, and had pups, and...

"Neya!"

"Yes, Mother!"

33

"Come help me wash the pups."

"Coming, Mother!"

"And remember, call me Fleek now. You are just about grown. It's time you used names."

"Yes, Fleek."

Neya and her litter-mates were not quite full grown, but already her mother had another litter. She was training Neya to care for them so that Fleek could fulfill her duties as the alpha female of the pack.

"First, wash the largest one. In this litter that's Belg. Wash his face, his ears, his paws, and don't forget to wash his back side."

"I know, Mo.. er Fleek."

Fleek sighed.

"Indulge me and allow me to tell you again. There won't be many more times."

Neya raised her ears up, to show her mother, or rather, to show the alpha female of the pack that Neya was listening.

"Your father, whom you are to call Scur from now on, will soon take me along when the pack goes hunting. He will expect me to attend all pack meetings and to help him keep the pack in line. As soon as these pups can eat meat and no longer need my milk, you will be their caregiver."

Neya understood. It had been the same when she was one of the weaned pups. Fon had taken over as her caregiver. Her mother had just been the alpha female of the pack, not paying Neya much attention at all, until she had decided to make Neya the caregiver of this litter.

"How soon will that be?"

"They will only need my milk for three more days."

Neya washed Belg as Fleek had directed, to show that she had been listening. It wasn't a bad duty to have. She actually enjoyed caring for the wolf-pups.

It reminded her of the vision she was now sure had been her future, though, and her thoughts soon returned to her dream mate. Clem was his name. He had brown, black, and white fur, instead of smoke-colored fur such as she and her wolf pack had. He would stand out in the desert, but he would blend in up here in the mottled shadows of the pine trees. He seemed to know how to fight. She wondered if he could hunt, but she was sure she could teach him, if need be. She already knew the ways of the hunter, even at nine months old.

"Mo.. er, Fleek?"

"Yes?"

"Will I have my own mate some day?"

"You might."

"How would that happen?"

"If a lone wolf leaves his pack and comes to claim you as his alpha female, then you and he could go off alone together and start your own pack. That is what your father and I did. The whole pack is our offspring. That is the way a pack is formed."

Neya wanted to ask her mother if her father had come to claim her first in a dream, but something made her hold back. Well, why kid herself. She knew what held her back.

Her mother, no, the alpha female of her pack would not approve of Neya's mate being mostly a "dog," and not a wolf like her father.

Did Neya need Fleek to approve her choice of mate, though?

Neya thought not.

She was still a child yet, but so was Clem. She guessed it would be six more moon cycles before Clem was grown. It would be three moon cycles before Neya was grown. For a while yet, they both needed their parents' protection.

Neya felt excitement, relief, and a little fear at the realization that, once they were both grown, if Clem came for her, then she would go.

CHAPTER 5: BUSINESS

Fortunately, my full bladder woke me up before my new human went off to work in the morning. Unfortunately, he wasn't awake yet. He might be mad if I woke him up, but the memories now told me he would be even madder if I urinated on his floor. This time, I decided to listen to the memories.

I reached out with my mind and found his mind. His sleeping mind was a calm blue, easy to penetrate. I wasn't sure that he would remember any mental movie I played in his dreams, so I suggested to him that he needed to wake up. I wasn't aware of knowing how to do that; I just did it as if I lived inside his body and was willing it to awake. I could tell once he no longer slept. His mind was more purple than blue, but still calm. I played him a mental movie of the two of us walking outside.

It was a short walk, but I did my business.

Sure enough, he was about to leave for the day without feeding me. I had to suggest that he fill my bowls: one with some of that dog food he had bought and promptly forgotten about, the other with water.

Dang!

I should have suggested he give me some of

the raw hamburger he had in the refrigerator! How stupid of me! Well, there was always this evening, after he came home. MMMmmmmmm! Now I had something to look forward to.

Finally, he left for work. I listened to make sure he got in his car and had driven a good ways away, out of human hearing distance, so that I was free to do my real business.

"Clem reporting for shut-in duty. My new human is out for the day."

Most of my 20 pack-mates' replies were distant, but they were all glad to hear from me and curious about my new human and home.

"Clem!"

"Heard you had an adventure!"

"Glad you're back, Buddy!"

"How's the new home?"

"We missed you!"

"Congratulations on finding a home so fast!"

"What's your new human like?"

"Is he kind?"

I told them how much I missed them, too, and how I wished I could be at the mine with them, but I was shut up in a little apartment without a doggie door. I answered all of their questions. Yep, I'd had an adventure, alright. I told them about my first car trip in the front seat in this life, and how I'd foolishly thought my parents' human was going to bond with me. I explained how I had been distracted with food and then abandoned.

A strange hush came over the pack when I told how I had felt the mind of the driver, and...

And then I was hushed, too.

I could not speak.

I didn't know why; I just couldn't.

The next thing I knew, Heg was on the other side of my new human's front door, telling me very quietly that I was never to speak aloud about feeling anyone's mind, seeing colors around minds, mental movies, or suggesting anything to anyone.

In fact, it was so quiet because Heg wasn't even speaking aloud. I knew he was there. I could hear him breathing. I could smell Heg's scent.

I was not hearing Heg's voice, though. Rather, I was seeing pictures in my mind that I knew Heg was putting there.

I saw myself sitting quietly where I was, not speaking. I saw myself putting pictures in another Kaxian's mind. (Wow! This works with our kind, too, and not just with humans!) I saw myself putting pictures in Niques' minds! (Whoa!) I again saw myself sitting quietly, not talking, only this time I was with Lido and Skil.

Wow!

First of all, whoa!

This works on Niques! I remembered the picture I had seen in my mind, back at the mine, of all of us as one big pack of wolves hunting prey that was tunneling. I wanted to ask Heg if he had put that picture there.

There it was again. I saw the picture in my mind again, only differently, from the perspective that Heg must have had when he put it there. But there was more. I saw the picture going into each human's mind, one by one. I saw it going into each miner's mind, and even each Nique's mind.

I let the surprise and delight that I felt exude from me, so that Heg would know my reaction. Some confusion seeped in to my emotional web, though. Why did he use pictures rather than mental movies? Why did Heg make his suggestions to one of us at a time? Now that I stopped to consider the idea, I was fairly certain that I could suggest to whoever was in my range, no matter how many that was, all at the same time. Couldn't Heg do that?

Apparently not, and without realizing it, in my confusion and desire to get answers, I must have broadcast a mental movie to Heg of myself suggesting to everyone in my range at once, because now I felt a surge of excitement from him.

Once more I saw a picture of myself not talking. Then followed another picture of me just with Heg. Then followed another of both of us not talking aloud. I understood: I was not to speak about the power of suggestion to anyone but him, and then only in our minds, so no one could hear.

"I understand."

I said it so quietly that even if my human were home, he wouldn't be able to hear me, but Heg could hear me through the door.

"Good. As for your new duties now that you are a shut-in, you will be a relay. Listen for messages with your name in them. If you hear one, then pass in on in the opposite direction."

"Got it. Is that all?"

"I have to go see some higher-ups about the other stuff we discussed. I am almost positive they will want me to train you in that."

Again, I got the image of me sitting near Lido and Skil, not talking to them.

"I understand. Heg?"

"Yeah?"

"I'm sorry about starting to talk earlier, about what should remain unsaid. Will there be trouble over it?"

I reached out gingerly to Heg's mind, and put a mental movie of me reaching out to my human's mind there, and then the mental movie of me talking to the pack earlier today.

"Sorry for what I said, Heg."

As soon as I sent the mental movie to Heg, his mind changed from calm cool blue to bright, excited pink. The pink pulsated, he was so excited. I hoped he would say something so we could enjoy the moment together. I was disappointed when he just answered my spoken question.

"You didn't know any better, and I didn't know your abilities had awoken, Clem. There won't be trouble this time, but you do not want to find out what happens when you do know better and you talk about this stuff. You are really young this time, to have so much responsibility, but you must keep this secret. It directly relates to command number one from Kax:

"No humans can know that dogs are aliens."

"Do you understand?"

"Yes, Heg, I understand."

I got a picture of Heg licking me on the head, and then I heard him running off.

***

Sitting in my new human's apartment all day was boring. I was grateful that I had a home and food and all, but I sure would have liked some toys to play with. I turned the TV on out of sheer boredom, but daytime TV is not that exciting, I've got to say. Oh, the old shows were OK, but watching all those commercials for medical treatments, scooters, and prescription drugs that had worse side effects than what they were treating was depressing! It made me feel sorry for humans. Who knew they were so frail? I turned the TV off.

I looked all over the little apartment for things to play with, but it was pretty empty and sterile. I knew better than to chew up any of my human's shoes, but my teeth were coming in and I sure missed the chew toys that my parents' human had provided. My new human's building was so new, there weren't even any mice or roaches to chase. Darn. I ran back and forth down the little hallway anyway, for exercise. I nosed the blinds aside so I could look out the windows, but there wasn't much to see from second story windows.

I had never been more bored. However, listening to all the messages being passed around by almost a thousand Kaxians within earshot kept me from being lonely.

"Berr: Ten Niques at Broash's mine."

A moment later, I heard Berr relay the message.

Finx: Cave in at Crawn's mine."

Sure enough, Finx relayed the message.

All the messages were about mining and guarding our mines from the Niques. I only spoke once, when I heard my name.

"Clem: Struck water at Fel's mine."

I relayed that one message, and then spent the rest of the day just listening to Kaxian business.

Well, I spent part of the time wondering what Heg would say to the higher-ups about my power of suggestion.

What kind of training would I get?

What duty would that prepare me to do?

Would I become a defense leader?

How, if I was stuck in this apartment?

And then I wondered what type of Kaxian duty my parents did. Were they relayers like I was now, or did they do something completely different? I prayed to Kax that they were happy and didn't miss me too much. Then, on impulse, I sent them a message.

"Banner and Queenie: your son Clem is alive and well in the apartment of a new human. He sends his love."

A little while later, I heard my name.

"Clem: your parents are well and happy to hear from you. They send their love."

***

Lido had dirt in his eyes. It was in his ears, too. He would never complain. Dirt in his eyes and ears meant no dirt in Skil's eyes or ears. No one that pretty should have dirt on her.

"Earth to Lido!"

"Pick up that dirt!"

"Wake up!"

Lido shook himself, and they all mock screamed at the dirt that flew off him onto them.

Lis said, "Come stand over here, Skil, so that he is at least looking toward the rest of us!"

Skil smiled and went to help Lis and Trixie pick up the dirt that Lido was throwing away from where Crash threw it as he mined the vein of jex.

Now Lido faced a new problem.

How could he move the dirt that got thrown on him without throwing it onto Skil? He concentrated so hard on only digging while Skil was away moving up the tunnel with dirt that he often threw dirt right in Lis and Trixie's faces.

"Hey! Watch it, Fatso!"

Lis started to dig dirt back at Lido, but Trixie nipped her leg to stop her.

"The tunnel is that way, Lis," Trixie said.

Lis growled at Trixie.

Trixie growled back.

Lis backed away.

"This is his fault, Trixie. Why are you mad at me?"

"Like I said, the tunnel is that way," Trixie said.

Skil sensed that everyone was getting agitated, so she tried to distract them all with news.

"Guess what?"

"Don't make us guess!"

"Just tell us, Skil!"

"All right. My humans are going to the pound this weekend to get another dog!"

"Wow!"

"I hope they don't get one of the Niques!"

"No, they need another working dog, to keep the coyotes out of our vinyard."

"Why don't they just fence the vinyard in?"

Skil looked at Lis with horror.

"Well, I know you couldn't come here to mine with us then, but really, I don't understand why they let you run off. A fence would fix that."

"Unless we just dug out like Clem did."

"Yeah, but look what happened to Clem."

"Yeah, so I am glad they can't afford to fence the vinyards."

"I guess it is cheaper to keep dogs than it is to build such a big fence."

"Yes, and we keep the birds and vermin away from the vines, too, not just the coyotes. They mostly come at night, so the humans don't miss me being gone days. The other Kaxians cover for me during the day."

"Wow, so do you know what kind of new dog your humans will get?"

"They said they're getting a male."

"Maybe they will get you a mate," Lis said.

Trixie gave Lis a scolding look.

Lis crinkled her eyebrows together in an expression of confusion in front of Trixie, but she let Skil see her sneering at Lido.

Lido lowered his head in sorrow.

Trixie nipped Lis in the rear, encouraging her to get back to work picking up dirt and moving it out of the tunnel.

Trixie moved over next to Lido and licked his shoulder.

"It only makes sense, Lido. Skil's mate would have to live with Skil at her humans' vinyard, in order to be a proper parent to her pups."

Lido howled in sadness, and then he ran out of   the   tunnel.

CHAPTER 6: MILLIE

The messaging system that we Kaxians copied millennia ago from the Niques is efficient and convenient. You humans know how it works, just not how vital it is:

When we urinate, we release a fluid that is scented with messages we have encrypted so that only our own team can decipher their meanings. Other Kaxians on our team pick up these messages and then reply. Niques try to cover up our messages with their own. On just one trip to the park, I can be in touch with my whole team of 20 Earthbound Kaxians.

The messaging system is dependent on the normal urinary functions of our physical dog bodies, though. We have not perfected the technology it would take to suppress the natural urinary functions of our physical bodies. We cannot turn off the messaging system when we can't get to the park.

"Bad dog!"

My new human was yelling at me and rubbing my six-month-old nose in the leakage on his bathroom floor. Never mind that he had left me alone inside his apartment for nine hours with no way of getting outside and no litter box. Yes, dogs can be trained to use litter boxes. We boy dogs just need litter boxes with high sides we can urinate against, is all.

Anyway, the stink is 100 times worse for me than it is for you, so you better believe I am just as interested in keeping it clean inside the den as you are.

I had held the urine inside for seven and a half hours, which is pretty darn good, if you ask me, and when I absolutely had to relieve myself, I had done so in the bathroom on the tile, not on the carpet. That self-control and consideration should have counted for something, if the world were a fair place. My human should have told me I was a good boy and petted me and been glad I had done my business in an area that was easy to clean.

The whole time he was yelling at me and rubbing my nose in my mess, I had been reaching out to his mind.

Yes!

Of course I thought of suggesting that he just clean this up and forget about it. That he go get me that hamburger from the refrigerator. But I got nothing.

I couldn't get anywhere close to his mind. It was wrapped up in a red cloud of frustration that he was choosing to express as anger. The Kaxian memories told me to show him that anger was the least useful expression of frustration.

Huh?

Kax!

This human is furious with me to the point of rubbing my nose in my urine, and you are telling me to somehow show him that anger is the least useful expression of frustration?

I need a practical way out of this situation, not philosophy!

I could tell that those memories were for dealing with other Kaxians. Yes, it would be a good idea to teach others to express their frustration in physical labor and industriousness, rather than anger. However, I figured the memories were useless to me in dealing with an angry human who would just as soon smash me as hear suggestions from me.

He was that angry.

I shut up the memories.

I needed a new tactic, if I was going to come out of this alright. I was going to have to do this my way. I thought for a split second on what had worked in the past, to mollify an angry human.

I looked up at my human and made my cutest puppy dog face while also making the crying noises in the back of my throat. Those crying noises almost always melt away a human's anger, especially when we are under a year old and at our cutest. I also tapped my tail ever so slightly on the floor, between my legs.

My human's phone rang.

He looked at it, and then his voice changed to sound soft and friendly when he answered.

"Hi Millie!"

I could hear Millie through the phone.

"Hi Randy! We're almost there! See you soon!"

"OK, great! See you soon, Millie!"

I tried taking advantage of the change in his voice to reach his mind, but the red cloud of frustration was still there, thick as ever, and he still smelled like anger. This was confirmed after he finished the call.

"Ugh!"

"Now I have to clean this up, and Millie will be here any minute!"

Still making the crying noises in the back of my throat, I got out of Randy's way. I could see only bad things happening if I stayed near him. I was beginning to think suggestion wouldn't ever work on a human who was already filled with a strong emotion, especially anger.

Determined to be helpful, I positioned myself so that I could guard the door when the visitors came.

Millie had said, **"We're** almost there."

Perhaps being muddled up in his cloud of frustration had kept Randy from noticing that Millie was bringing someone with her. I thought he should be more on guard, but he was upset, so I figured I better be on guard for him. Humans like their pets to be helpful. They praise us for that more often than anything else, except obedience.

If Millie had come by herself, I might still be with Randy.

But no, she had to show up with one of the Niques!

Millie's little dog was a red Pomeranian who had come to one of our other mines before. He was pretty snooty, too. From his perch in her arms, he started with the insults the minute she walked in the door.

"Ha ha! Someone had an accident!"

"Ya Think?"

I knew this sarcastic comment was childish and stupid of me, but he was just so annoying and rude. He didn't stop there, either.

"Everyone knows humans can't stand the smell of the messaging system! Leave it to a Kaxian to act as if you just got off the ship yesterday!"

"Very funny, and everyone knows you Niques move in on territory that has already been claimed."

"Since when!"

"You are moving in on my territory right now! This is my human's den. You don't belong here, just as all you Niques moved in on Earth after we had already laid our claim."

"Says who!"

Ooh!

I was beginning to see my own red cloud of frustration. The memories told me he was baiting me to make me lose control so he could get me in trouble with the humans. "Calm down," the memories cautioned. "Anger is the least useful expression of frustration," they reminded me.

It was too late.

My fuse was already lit.

My puppy self had a short fuse, too.

"Come on down from there and let's see who thinks he's so smart!"

"Nah. I'm happy where I am, thanks."

"Chicken."

"Am not!"

As fate would have it, that is when Randy decided he wanted to hold Millie's hand. To him, our insults and threats just sounded like wolves barking at each other.

"Millie, how about putting your dog on the floor for a while?"

Millie was paying more attention to us.

"All right, but I have to stay with him. It

doesn't sound like he is getting along with your dog."

Randy glared at me furiously, as if it was my fault that Millie's little dog had such bad manners.

I tried to appease my human by lowering my head, tail, ears, and eyes, looking at the floor.

And then Millie addressed her dog.

"Snookems, why don't you play with the other nice doggie for Mommie, huh?"

Laughing as hard as I could, I said, "Yeah, Snookems, come play with me!"

Millie sat down on the couch and put Snookems on the floor under her legs, where he stayed and cowered. My human sat next to Millie on the couch, and the two of them proceeded to make goo goo eyes at each other.

Snookems could not leave well enough alone. He had to taunt me from his little fort under his human's legs.

"Ha ha!"

Snookems peeked out from one side of his human's legs.

I ran around the coffee table.

"You can't get me!"

He knocked a box of tissues off the coffee table and peeked out from the other side.

I ran around to the other side, but I knocked some magazines down with my tail as I hurried by. Coincidentally, they landed right in front of Snookems, blocking my way to him. I looked up at the humans to see if they noticed, but they were looking at a magazine together, pointedly trying to ignore us. Snookems still wouldn't shut up.

"And I say 'tough luck' to you Kaxians, on making the first trade claim on Planet Earth."

I should have known what caution was. I blame the six-month-old dog body. I could not keep quiet. I simply had to retort to every one of Snookems' taunts.

"Oh! Come on! You Niques are just too lazy to go explore the galaxy and find your own source of jex! And you are always hiding behind your humans while you taunt us like the babies you resemble. Come out of there, you little rat dog!"

The humans were pretty much oblivious to our argument, which after all just sounded to them like two dogs barking at each other, until Snookems started lying.

"Help! Millie, help me! This bully big dog is going to hurt me!"

"You are such a liar, calling out to your human when you know I can't..."

Millie wriggled out from under Randy's arm, picked her little Snookems up, and started in again with the baby talk.

"Ooh! Is my little Snookems scared?"

She put his nose right up to her nose, and nuzzled him like a mamma would nuzzle her pup.

"There, there, Boy."

She pet the top of his head the way a momma licks her pup.

"Mommy will protect you."

I was right in the middle of growling out what a chicken Snookems was when Randy grabbed me by the collar, pulled me into the kitchen, and grabbed a frying pan to hit me with.

"Nooooo!" Millie screamed.

She ran in to stop Randy from hurting me.

He said, "This mutt is going straight to the

pound! I only got him so your Snookems would have someone to play with. It looks like he has no idea how to play nice with others!"

"I'll take him," Millie said, "I'll take him right now."

"Noooooooooo, don't go!"

Randy said this in a whiny voice that hurt my ears. I put my paws over my ears and looked over at Snookems. His paws were over his ears, too. We winced together, commiserating at our aching ears. Randy didn't notice, in fact he whined even more.

"We can put him in the bedroooooooom and..."

"I am not leaving that poor animal alone with you, Randy Loosk! I don't even like big dogs, but I care more about him than you do, and supposedly he's your dog!"

'Yeah,' I thought, 'what she said!'
***

Skil took her turn getting dirt thrown on her for the first time since she met Lido. It wasn't so bad. He hadn't needed to go out of his way to protect her from it. Still, she wished he were here, just so she could see him and hear his voice. she threw the dirt extra hard whenever she was passing it to Lis.

Trixie felt bad for Skil, but she had to be the grown-up here.

"I miss Lido, too, Skil, but let's not make our job more difficult than it has to be. Try and keep your dirt pile neat."

"Yes, Ma'am."

Skil shuddered over her memories of the messages in the relay after Lido had run off yesterday.

"Lido is over in the west district."

"Tell him to get his behind back to Heg's mining site!"

"Niques in the west district!"

"Lido chased the Niques from the west district!"

"Lido was picked up by the dog catcher."

CHAPTER 7: BIG DOG ROOM

I spent that night in one of the thirty five-by-ten chain-link kennels in the big-dog room at the pound, hoping I wouldn't have to start out in yet another body in the next couple days. Being a puppy is hard work.

At least I was with a bunch of fellow Kaxians. All thirty kennels were full. I had plenty of company. In most ways, I liked being in the pound more than I liked being abandoned.

"Hey, Clem!"

"Aw, they got you, too, Lido?"

"Yeah."

Like everyone else in the room, I needed to convince a human to adopt me and take me home with him or her. I was up against some formidable competition from fellow Kaxians: a dozen pet-me's and ten go-get-its, both types that are perennially popular with the humans.

Like I said before, I am mostly a Queensland Heeler this time around. It's not the cutest breed of dog, and that is what you want to be if you are competing for the attention of the limited number of humans who come into the pound to adopt pet dogs.

It might seem like we would all want to be out in the wild, hunting for our food and doing whatever we want. Well, I had a chance to do that, and aside from that weird dream I had about the she-wolf, it was not at all appealing. It just seemed lonely.

Besides, living with humans is what keeps us Kaxians covert. (Yeah, it hides the Niques' alien origins, too, but who cares about them?) Living with humans has worked well for millennia, and besides, it is tradition. Have you ever tried to buck tradition? If you have, then you know what I mean when I say, don't try it.

It doesn't really matter if I agree or not, though. Remaining covert is command number one, straight from Kax:

No humans can know that dogs are aliens.

We have the technology to be born again and again and again, so mortal peril is no excuse to blow our cover and allow any human to guess we are not from Earth. Being in the pound is no excuse, either. Besides, every Kaxian (and every Nique, too, but who cares about them?) wants to be reborn. The punishment for blowing our cover is we don't get to be reborn.

OK.

So you see the challenge that was before me?

We Australian Cow Dogs can jump really high and run really fast, but how many humans are looking for those qualities when they pick out a pet? Not many, that's how many.

Nope, I had to concentrate on being responsive to what the humans said, and I had to pray to Kax they noticed how attentive I was.

Of course we didn't want any of the Niques to be adopted, so we worked together to keep the humans in our big-dog room at the pound, choosing just among us Kaxians.

As soon as the pound opened up for business in the morning, a small human boy ran in.

"Dad! Dad! Look at all the dogs, Dad!"

He ran down the aisle and back, looking each of us in the eye as he passed by.

"Can we take them all home with us?"

He kept running up and down the aisle of kennels, stopping here and there to put his fingers through the holes to pet one of us, or to let us lick his hands.

"Don't put your fingers in the cages!"

The boy's father was more frightened than angry, but he was letting his frustration at being frightened manifest itself as anger.

"These dogs might bite you! We don't know which ones are friendly."

The boy was used to his father's temper, and knew just what tone to make with his voice, to appease him.

"Aw, Dad, they're all friendly. None of them are going to bite me. They're all sad about being in these cages. I want to let them all out."

"Sorry, Son, you can't do that."

The father hugged the boy.

"Let's just look at them all in their cages and see if one might be the one we want to take home."

We were all talking again, of course.

"I'm friendly!"

"I'm more friendly!"

"I like to play!"

"I want to come home with you and play!"

You know what? I almost think the boy understood us. He sure seemed to run to each of us right after we spoke, and to answer what we were saying.

"Oh! You are friendly, aren't you?"

"Yes, you are friendly, too, huh?"

"Do you like to play with a ball?"

When he came to my kennel, I barked out my answers to each of his questions, of course, but I also smiled at him, with my lips pulled back to show my teeth and my tongue sticking out and my ears up. I wagged my tail fast, too, in a show of enthusiasm. I was doing all I could to show the boy I was a happy, friendly dog who would play with him. I was also trying my new trick of reaching out with my mind to connect to his mind, but his mind was swollen with excitement and pity. There was no room in there for my suggestions. I kept trying.

The boy took a rubber frog out of his pocket, to show me. I slanted my head sideways to show I was looking at the toy in fascination. Humans love it when we do that.

"Would you go and get this for me, Boy? You wouldn't chew it up, would you?"

"I would be happy to go get it for you, and of course I wouldn't chew it up!"

The boy laughed and tossed the toy into my kennel. I dutifully got it and brought it back to him, holding it in the front of my mouth for him to take.

Laughing, the boy was reaching to get the rubber frog back when his father saw him and came storming over.

"I told you not to put your hand inside the

cages! OK, I can see you're not going to listen, so you'll have to wait in the car while I pick a dog for us to take home."

The boy started crying then, still looking at his little toy frog that I held in my mouth, ready for him to take.

"But Dad! He has my frog!"

"Well you should have listened when I told you not to reach into the cages. You could have been bitten! I need to be able to trust that you will do as you are told. Your punishment is to wait in the car while I choose the dog myself. I'm sorry, but you disobeyed me, and that is not acceptable."

The dad came back after he put his son in the car, but of course he was particularly upset at the sight of his son's toy frog in my cage, sitting there reminding him of his son's disobedience. He was far too emotional for my suggestive abilities to work on him. I couldn't even play the dad a mental movie of him calmly explaining the rules of a new place to the boy, before they entered the next new place, let alone of the dad picking me to take home with them.

Too bad.

I liked that boy, and I think he liked me.
***

Several adoption failures later, a young couple walked in, and I could tell they were going to take a dog home with them that day. It was just a question of which one of us would be the "lucky" one. What really caught my notice, though, was Skil's scent on them. These were Skil's humans!

Lido looked at me at the same time as I looked at him.

"Are those Skil's humans?"

"Yep," Lido told me, "She said they were planning on getting another dog."

Lido raised his eyebrows three times at me, and then turned to face the humans, wagging his tail.

I tried reaching out to the humans' minds, but they, too, were full of excitement and pity, just as the little boy's mind had been. I wasn't having any luck, but I kept trying.

These humans spoke softly and moved slowly. They stopped at the first cage, where as soon as the woman looked at him, a shaggy, untrimmed, standard black poodle rolled over onto his back and begged to have his belly rubbed. (Don't ask me how standard Kaxian poodles are related to toy Nique poodles. I really don't want to think about that!) The poodle wagged his tail at the nice couple, full of hope and encouragement.

The rest of us all started talking at once:

"Pick me!"

"Oh, choose me!"

"I'm a good girl!"

"I want to go home with you!"

Of course, the humans just heard a bunch of barking that was so loud they couldn't hear each other speaking. I liked these humans, though. They both smiled when we all started talking to them.

The man said to his mate, "Enthusiastic, aren't they!"

The man's mate smiled, nodded her head, and looked around at us all.

"Oh, look, Dear. Look at how lovable this poodle is."

"Yes, he is crying out to be petted, isn't he?"

"I can't explain it, but I feel almost compelled

to pet him, right through the bars of this cage!"

"Heh! Yes, I agree, he is downright compelling."

The man smiled at his mate.

She said, "I suppose we should look at all the dogs, though."

"Yes, and don't forget we mostly are getting a dog for protecting the vinyard. Wanting to be petted is nice, but we need a dog who will make intruders think twice."

"I suppose, Honey."

Well, that did it. Most of us started trying to look tough, now: standing up straight, or pacing back and forth like lions inside our cages. It is difficult to look tough on intruders without looking scary to one's potential humans, though. Try it sometime.

The Rottweiler in the next cage took toughness to the extreme, growling and snarling so much that the female human almost fainted. Her mate took her hand and helped her quickly pass the Rottweiler by.

My friend Lido the portly bulldog was in the next kennel they came to. He played it a little smarter, not growling or snarling, but standing up straight and alert. He spoke to Skil's male human in a businesslike voice.

"I'll watch your vinyard for you,"

The man seemed pleased.

"Well now, you seem like an alert fella."

"Oh no, George. Look how, um, big he is. He will eat us out of house and home!"

I prayed to Kax for a chance to help my friend Lido. Thank Kax, Skil's female human looked right at me when she turned away from Lido. She was focused on me, and her mind was temporarily open.

I looked over at Lido, wagged my tail, and played her a mental movie that suggested Lido was the best dog there. I showed him standing out, superimposed in front of all the other dogs. I emphasized his strong protective build, yet showed him being lovable and cuddly with her mate and her.

She smiled and turned back to Lido.

"Well hey there. Are you a good boy?"

"I am the best there is, Ma'am."

"Will you watch over us and our vinyard, and keep us safe?"

"It would be an honor, Ma'am."

Her mate had wandered down the aisle.

"George! This is the dog I want after all!"

Lido danced around in circles in his cage, wagging his tail so fast you couldn't see it.

"I owe you one, Clem! Anything you want! Anything you ever want for the rest of our days on Earth!"

"Aw Lido, we're best friends. You don't owe me anything. This is just what best friends do, help each other."

Lido's new humans went off to fill out the paperwork.

Lido sat down to wait, wearing the biggest grin any bulldog ever wore.

***

Next, a middle-aged couple of humans walked into our big-dog room. They looked at each of us in turn, making little comments on what they thought.

The memories help me at times like these, and I can mimic human expressions. Yes, I can!

OK, and after 98 lives, I know most of the

common human commands already, so I know how to make humans happy. Most of the time. When my puppy body doesn't have an accident and I am with an actual dog person who is not just using me to impress a female.

Hoo boy.

When they came up to my kennel, I looked at the humans with the saddest human-like facial expression I could manage. I made my ears droop. I let my mouth go slack so that my lips hung down. I really laid it on thick with the body language, too: tail tip just barely tapping hopefully, sitting down with my shoulders hunched and head ducked, puppy eyes looking up at them expectantly.

"Aw, look at this one."

"Wow, he looks sad."

"I'll say! You would think he knew he was in the pound."

"Yeah, it's like he is begging us to take him home."

"How could he possibly know what the pound is?"

"Maybe he can smell something."

"Oh yeah. Dogs have a really good sense of smell. Some people say it is 100 times as powerful as a human's sense of smell."

Wow! They really knew a lot about us 'dogs.' That was nice. That meant they were dog people who would probably make a good home for us. I started daydreaming about what their home was like, and I almost missed the next thing they said. Good thing I heard it with at least part of my attention.

"I wonder if he always looks sad like that, though. That would be depressing."

Uh oh!

Time to show them I can be a fun-loving guy, too. I stood up and wagged my tail happily, put my ears up in a jaunty way, hung my tongue out of my mouth in the expression humans call a smile, and danced around in a circle.

"Wow!"

"Yeah!"

"Look how happy he looks now!"

"It's as if he understood what we said!"

"Did you understand us, Boy?"

"Yep, I did. I understand every word you say."

Even more, I understand what your body language is saying, even if you don't intend your body to say things. I can tell when humans are lying, just by their posture. If you humans would pay attention to your own body language, you would know this, too. You watch our body language much more closely than you watch each other's. Why is that?

Anyway, I wanted out of this kennel, like, yesterday.

I wagged my tail emphatically, including my bottom in the wag so that my whole body shook with happiness that they were talking to me. I made the crying noises in the back of my throat. Still sitting down, I inched my whole body closer and closer to my kennel door, the door that stood between me and these two friendly humans.

The woman gestured for the man to follow her outside the room.

Silly human. Didn't she know I could have heard them even if they left the building and talked in their vehicle? They just went out into the hallway.

"I can tell you really like that last one, don't

you?"

"Yeah, I do."

"I do, too," she said, "But I don't really know why!"

"I think it's because he seems to really be in tune with us. I doubt he can really understand what we say, but it seems like he is really good at reading our body language and knowing what we want him to do. I like obedience in a dog."

"Well, do you want to get him?"

"Yeah, let's get him!"

Woo Hoo!

I did my own happy dance inside my kennel. I was going home with my new humans! I had finally convinced some humans to pick me!

Really, that should have been it, but then the Niques did something sneaky.

CHAPTER 8: PIG IN SPANISH

My humans went to the front room of the pound, the one with the big counter, to fill out my adoption paperwork. I was pleased with these humans. They spoke softly to me, like they cared about me. They weren't going to leave me alone for nine hours without any way to relieve myself.

I could tell the man was a real dog person. He was going to take me for walks every day and play with me and pet me and let me sleep in the same room with him. I just knew it.

His female was supportive of him. She wanted him to have a dog so that he would be happy. She would help him remember to feed me and make sure I always had water.

Yep, I was getting a great new home! In return, I would learn any new commands they taught me the first time they said them. I would come right away when they called me. I would watch them whenever they were in the room with me, to see if they wanted me to do anything.

I would also conduct my Kaxian business, of course, whatever that turned out to be. That was my main priority and the whole reason I was here on Earth, but I was ready to think of these new humans as my family. I already loved them. I thought they would come to love me, too.

Once my humans left our big-dog room and walked down the hall a ways, they were out of my suggestion range. I could see, in my newly discovered "mind's eye," their happy blue minds as they walked out, and then these gradually faded away from my mental sight.

I could hear one of the little dogs, the Niques, panting in the front-counter room. I heard my humans walking in there. When my humans walked past where the Nique was panting, I heard them change direction to walk over and wait behind a bunch of other humans who were lined up at the counter. I could hear my new humans waiting in that line.

"Wow! I am so excited we found a dog to adopt!" the woman said, getting into the line.

"I know! Do you think he looks like a pig?"

What? I look like a pig? I wasn't sure if I liked that!

"Yeah! I thought it was only me, but he does look like a pig! Want to name him 'Piggy'?"

"No, I don't like 'Piggy'."

The line moved up and they advanced toward the counter.

The woman asked a lady in front of her, "Hey, how do you say 'pig' in Spanish?"

"You won't like it," the lady said.

"No? Try us, please."

"'Pig' in Spanish is 'puerco'."

"You're right; I don't like that."

"I don't either," said the man.

Thank Kax!

I would be the laughing stock of every Kaxian ever (and every Nique, too, but who cares about them?), for all my lives, if I had to be called 'Puerco'!

Do I really look like a pig?

I turned and looked at my hindquarters, which admittedly did look a little porcine. I looked at my snout, I mean my mouth, in the reflection in my water dish.

Hm! I guess I do look a little like a pig!

Please don't call me 'Piggy'.

Please!

I heard my humans get to the front of the line where they were handed a bunch of forms to fill out. They accepted all the forms the woman handed them without questioning what they were for. I knew their peril because I could hear the rest of the humans talking.

"Wow! There sure are a lot of people entering the lottery to win the chihuahua!"

"Yeah, look, that couple even just came out of the big-dog room and took an entry form."

"Well, the chihuahua is awfully cute! Did you see all the tricks it can do?"

"Yes! I really want it!"

"Me, too!"

I have never felt so frustrated in all my 99 lives. These were MY humans! I had them ready to take me home, and I could hear the enemy in the little dog room, gloating.

"Priox, this is the best placement for you."

"Intel has it you will have half an acre whenever you tell them you need to go outside!"

"We've got this rigged. They will win the raffle and take you home."

"How do you big dogs like them apples!"

"Ha ha!"

"Your humans are so stupid they just entered a raffle for a dog they haven't even seen!"

"We're going to prevail, Kaxians. Just you wait and see."

"We will get all the best placements!"

"It will be our jex going from Earth, not yours!"

"Yeah, because when it comes right down to it, we Niques are smarter. Uh huh!"

I so wanted to go over there and show those little dogs how much difference being smarter makes in close quarters, against someone who is much bigger! I confess, I imagined myself looming up on one of them inside his kennel. He was cringing in fear because I was so big and he was so small. Let's see how smart he thought he was then, huh?

But what would happen then? This new six-month-old dog body would be put down, is what.

No thanks.

My mind went into overdrive, thinking of a way out of this mess.

What if I played a mental movie to all the humans within my suggestion range? What would I play for them?

I really wanted one of them to go tear up all those forms that my new humans were filling out to enter the lottery to win that stupid chihuahua, thanks to the Niques' scheming.

Oddly, the mental movie for what I wanted started making itself in my mind. I noticed that my movie had a red tint to it, but I didn't waste time trying to guess what that meant.

In my mental movie, my humans were smiling and chatting with each other as they sat on a green pad on an old fashioned wooden bench in the front room of the pound, filling out the raffle paperwork. They stopped talking when they saw my three affected humans storming down the hall toward them.

The three affected humans, two males and a female, were moving fast. Their faces were contorted, with their noses all scrunched up and their teeth showing. The three of them grabbed the papers out of my humans' hands and started tearing them up. They tore violently, and they were growling.

My male human slowly rose in front of his mate, protecting her behind him. She cowered in fear. He looked afraid, too, but also determined. One of his hands went up diagonally in front of his face, and the other went out diagonally in front of his chest.

A female human coming down the hall from the other side of the building saw all this for the chaos that it was, and called the police on her cell phone...

I shook myself.

OK, that scenario was not going to work.

I didn't think the people affected by my mental movie would notice anything weird about whatever I had suggested they do. However, most of the humans in the building were outside my range. Most of those inside my range were full of excitement and pity, so my mental movie would not reach them. Also, new people were entering the building at random times.

I would have to choose a single target for a mental movie, and the movie would have to show the human something unremarkable to do, in order to stop my humans from adopting that stupid chihuahua instead of me.

I couldn't risk blowing our cover as pet dogs rather than space alien Kaxians and creating a major incident. No, that was not happening. I wanted to be reborn again, thank you very much.

I closed my physical eyes and used my mind's eye to scan the human minds inside my range. Most of them were pink with excitement or orange with excitement combined with pity.

Ooh! There was a calm blue mind. One of the pound employees was walking down the hall toward the big-dog room.

Perfect!

Now, what did I want her to do in order to stop my humans from entering that stupid raffle? Well, OK, it was simple, really.

I honed in on her calm blue mind. I started making a mental movie of her going over to ask my humans a friendly question:

"Hi! How's the paperwork going, for the chihuahua raffle?"

But it wasn't necessary for me to play my mental movie for her. Kax had blessed me with good humans who were kind. I could hear them talking about me while they waited in that stupid line the little dogs had fabricated to trap them into taking one of them home, instead of me.

"Well, we might as well go talk to him while we wait for our turn back at the counter."

"Yeah. There's really no need to wait here."

"Right! All these people are going to take a while."

Yes! I couldn't help barking out a gloat of my own, I was so happy! My fellow big dogs from Kax joined in.

"Ha ha!"

"Your little trick failed!"

"The humans are coming back here into our room!"

***

Neya crouched in the grass beneath a huge pine tree, bristling with new feelings as she listened to one of the old stories that her mother... no, that Alpha Female Fleek was telling the litter of wolf pups that she would soon leave in Neya's care.

"A long time ago, before anyone whose name we know was born, hundreds of big stars fell out of the sky and landed on the ground."

"Did they catch the forest on fire?"

"Did they make loud noises, like thunder?"

"Good questions! But, no, and no. The big stars landed on the ground without any noise at all. They were being driven here, in the way that humans drive cars and trucks on their roads."

"We are not to cross the roads!"

"The humans might smash us with their cars and trucks!"

"Were humans driving the big stars?"

"Right, Belg! We are not to cross the roads. Yes, Ordn, we don't cross the roads because the humans might crush us with their cars and trucks. Good guess, Tolt! But no, the humans were not driving the big stars.

"The big stars landed on the ground silently. We wolves gathered far away to watch. They smelled like metal because they were made of metal. They opened up, and dog aliens came out."

"What are dog aliens?"

"Dog aliens look a bit like wolves. They walk like wolves. They talk like wolves, too, but they are not wolves. They came from the stars long before anyone whose name we know was born."

"Are the dog aliens our friends?"

"Will we see the dog aliens?"

"Where are the dog aliens?"

This was the part Neya had been dreading. She had heard this story hundreds of times in her nine months of life. The wolves considered it a vital part of history, not to be unknown or ever forgotten.

"No, Kess. The dog aliens are not our friends. We don't trust them. Yes, Ordn. We do see the dog aliens sometimes. Tolt, the dog aliens live with humans, as their pets. That is the easiest way to know it is a dog alien coming, when you smell one. They smell like humans."

"Do they really look like wolves?"

"Why don't we trust them?"

"Belg, all dog aliens look at least a little like wolves. Some are bigger than us. Some are smaller. Some of their bodies have odd shapes. Some of their ears hang down. The biggest difference is in their coloring. They don't all blend in with the desert. Some do, but most stand out so you can see them from miles away. They almost all smell like humans, and that is the easiest way to tell that you are dealing with a dog alien and not a wolf."

"Do..."

"Wait."

"OK."

"Kess, we don't trust the dog aliens because

they are not of our world. Earth is not their mother, the way she is our mother. The moon does not rule them the way he rules us, as our father."

Neya tried very hard not to show her feelings as Fleek sternly examined all the pups' faces to make sure they all understood:

Dogs are aliens, and they are not our friends.

We don't trust the dog aliens.

CHAPTER 9: DOG BOND

"There's our pig dog!" the man said, with a fond smile on his face.

Oh no!

Please don't name me 'Piggy'!

Please!

I tried reaching into their minds to suggest they not name me something so ridiculous, but their minds were too full of emotions: purple joyous excitement, mostly.

The woman smiled back at her mate as the pound employee unlocked my kennel, put my leash on, and handed it to the man.

"Here, Boy!" the man said.

I was being as friendly as I knew how when I walked up to my new human: hanging my tongue out of my mouth, holding my ears up high, and wagging my tail in as big a movement as I could.

My new human, Scott, looked friendly, too. He was smiling and slightly bent over so that we could see eye to eye.

When I got within his reach, he petted me for the first time, saying,

"Yes, Boy, you're coming home with us. Yes, you   are!"

79

I licked his hand.

He smiled and pet me some more.

And then...

All thought of entering Scott's mind to suggest anything at all went away. I had been trying over and over, ever since he called me their pig dog, to get him to forget that name, to please not name me "Piggy!" Now, I didn't care if he named me that. I completely forgot my plan to have him not name me "Piggy." That plan was erased from my mind, and anything at all that I had been thinking was replaced by a new idea.

This man was my human! He thought of me as being his dog, but he was my human. I was responsible for him. I felt fiercely protective of him.

I also wanted my human to be happy. I would do whatever it took to make him happy. I would obey any command he gave me. If he named me 'Piggy', I would no longer even mind (at least not when he was around).

I knew all of this within the time it took our eyes to twinkle as they met when he smiled at me, after I licked his hand.

That was it.

We bonded!

This man was my human.

I was his dog.

I would serve him until death parted us.

I would die for him.

More, I could feel that my loyalty had completely changed. Not more than a moment had passed, but deep down inside I knew that I would fight any of my fellow Kaxians, even, to defend my human. I would go wherever my human said, do whatever he told me to do, and enjoy it.

In the back of my mind, I still knew I was a Kaxian. I remembered my former life of wishing for promotion and looking forward to mining. Those days were over.

One tiny corner of my mind was intensely curious how I could still serve Kax, how any Kaxian could still serve Kax, under the dog bond. This part of my mind was so tiny that I could easily ignore it. I did ignore it. I was ecstatic to be on a leash, walking down the hallway of the pound with my new human. Nothing else mattered.

The pound employee led us all into a clinic. Thank Kax for sending me memories of what would happen next. Otherwise, I might have been afraid. Instead, I was just giddy with excitement at getting such good new humans!

"OK, he is your dog now, so you hold him while we give him his shots."

The woman held me while the man petted me. I was so content, I barely felt the shots.

"Oh!" The woman said when they shot the identifier chip into the skin on the top of my head,

"Did you have to do that? It looked like it really hurt him!"

Such compassion, and she wasn't even bonded with me! I knew I had been right about her! She was going to be one of my best humans ever, and furthermore, she wasn't even a dog person.

I smelled a cat's scent on her. It was on my male human, too, but it was strong on her. The cat was hers. She was a cat person. That was fine. I also smelled two other dogs on my new humans: a Nique and a Kaxian, but their scents were faint. I would be the only dog in their den, which I would also share with a cat.

The pound employee said, "Don't worry. Dogs are very forgiving. He won't hold that against you."

My human's mate crumpled her eyebrows at the pound employee, and then looked into my eyes.

"I am so sorry, Boy. I didn't know they were going to do that. Do you forgive me?"

"Of course I forgive you."

She couldn't possibly understand Kaxian speech, but I licked her hand and then smiled at her, to try and get the point across.

She smiled at me and petted me, and I knew things were going to be great in my new home.

Just then, another pound employee came running into the room.

"Scott and Cherise Kelley?"

"Yes, that's us," my new human's mate said.

"You need to come to the front office!"

***

Lido usually enjoyed car rides, but this time he was just impatient to get there, already, and see Skil. Part of him could not believe he had pulled this off. He was afraid to look forward to seeing Skil when he arrived, for fear it was all a mistake and they were taking him someplace he would never see her again.

Oh, this looked good!

They turned off the main highway and headed down a long dirt road that ran between rows of trellised grape vines. A few houses sat at the end of the dirt road, but no other houses were in sight. The grape vines stretched off into the distance until small rolling hills ended the view at the sky.

It was a few hours yet till dark, so Skil was still at the mine. Lido looked for her anyway.

Oh.

Wow.

There was her scent.

It was all over the place. He breathed deeply, savoring Skil's scent and letting it keep him company until he saw her.

The car stopped in front of the houses.

Eight Kaxians milled around near the car: four German shepherds, three Rottweilers, and a American Staffordshire terrier . Some wagged their tails to greet their humans. Most kept looking askance at Lido's door.

The male human opened Lido's door and snapped a leash to his collar.

"Come, Boy! Let me show you around."

"Let him show you around, New Guy, but just know I am your actual boss around here."

Keeping quiet so that his new human would not become alarmed, Lido bowed his head to acknowledge the Rottweiler as pack leader.

The pack leader hung back, standing still and proud with a female Rottweiler who Lido figured was his mate. The third Rottweiler smelled like he was their son, and stayed near them.

"Boss, the new guy looks young. Will he go to the mines with Skil, or stay here?"

"We'll see how well he fits in, Blackie, and then I'll decide."

Lido tore his attention away from the other Kaxians to look up at his new human and wag his tail, to show he was happy to be here.

The human petted Lido once on the head and

then walked him the entire perimeter of the vinyard. The four German shepherds and the American Staffordshire terrier walked along with them, milling all about and running off to chase birds as they went. Every time one of them chased a bird off the vines, the human said:

"Good Boy!" or

"Good Girl!"

They finished touring the perimeter of the vinyard, and then it was time to eat. Their male human let Lido off the leash, and their female human brought out a bag of dog food.

Lido waited to see which bowl was his.

"Here, Boy, your dish is here."

She indicated a bowl next to Blackie's. Lido let Blackie get to his bowl first, just so there was no misunderstanding about anyone trying to eat someone else's food.

"Come on, Boy! Eat your food!"

But then Lido heard the voice he had been longing to hear.

"Lido! Is that really you? How did you get here? Are you here to stay? I can't believe it!"

Skil came running through the vinyards on her way home from the mine, talking the whole time until she was right there, and she tackled him. The two of them went rolling around play fighting to use up some of the energy they both felt at being together again after two whole days apart.

After the humans went back in the house and all the Kaxians were finished eating, Boss called a meeting.

Lido sat down next to Skil. He noticed that Blackie moved over quickly to also sit next to her.

"Alright, so by now, everyone knows that the new guy is Lido from Skil's mining pack. Let's welcome him to our vinyard pack."

"Welcome, Lido!

"Hey Lido!"

"Glad to have you with us."

"Lido, our humans have us here to protect them and their grape vines. If we don't do that, then we will all be back at the pound."

The pack members had strong feelings about going back to the pound.

"Don't wanna go back there!"

"No way, no how!"

"Right, so we may be able to send both you and Skil to the mine during the day, but that doesn't mean you won't still have to do vine guard duty in the evening. Skil already does double duty. She doesn't have time for much else but duty, eating, and sleeping."

"I don't mind, Boss."

Blackie said something meant for only Skil to hear, but Lido heard it, and it made all the hair on his back stand on end.

"I wish you had time to play with me like you were playing with the new guy."

Lido looked at Skil. She was looking at Blackie with her head slanted to the side, as if she was trying to figure out what he meant. The meaning was all too clear to Lido, but it was Skil's choice who she played with. He was just sad at the thought of her playing with any male other than him.

Boss continued the meeting.

"So, we need to figure out how to get all the runs covered, and whether or not that leaves us free to send two Kaxians to the mine. I would like to do that, so let's do our best to cover all the runs. Skil!"

"Yes, Boss?"

"You take Lido on the sunset run."

"Yes, Boss!"

Lido didn't hear the rest of the meeting. He was too happy wallowing in the realization he would be running the vinyards with Skil soon.

Blackie didn't take it well. He paced back and forth during the entire meeting.

Blackie's pacing was the one thing Lido did pay attention to at the meeting. He felt the Rottweiler's eyes on him, and it didn't feel good.

Finally, Lido was running the vinyard with Skil. It was even more fun than mining together. They were free to run and play, and they did. Not too much play, but every once in a while one of them would tackle the other, and the two of them would go rolling over each other, play fighting.

Skil had explained to Lido what they were supposed to be doing.

"It's simple, really. The humans set this place up well, with the houses in the center of the vinyard. The rest of us sleep there. Our duty is to patrol. We wake them up if trouble comes."

"Wow, that's pretty easy."

"Yep!"

"Does trouble ever come?"

"Yeah, the coyotes have been here twice."

Still, for some reason, the two of them just could not keep from tackling each other and play fighting. It was the best time Lido remembered ever having, at least in his limited memories of only this life.

***

Blackie had trouble sleeping that night, even after his human came out and petted him goodnight. He tried to get comfort from his father, the leader of his pack.

"Boss?'

"Yeah, Blackie?"

"Now that we have the new guy, could Skil maybe just stay here and run the vinyard with me?"

Boss sighed and licked Blackie's nose.

"I know you like Skil, Son."

Blackie's tail started wagging.

"Hold on."

Blackie's tail stopped wagging.

"I know you like her, but I can't promise her to you, Son. I have to send her to the mine, and I will probably have to send Lido, too."

"But Dad!"

Boss gave Blackie a stern look.

"Sorry. But Boss..."

"I can see that I haven't done my Kaxian duty by you, Blackie. I've been too busy being Boss of this vinyard pack, and not busy enough being your father."

Blackie stood up and shook himself.

"Never mind. Every time I try and talk to you, you just say a bunch of mumbo jumbo about duty. I'll figure it out for myself. Thanks for nothing."

Blackie ran off into the dark hills alone.

CHAPTER 10: PUPPY ROOM

My humans were going to the front-counter room again. I had just been elated at bonding with my new human and finding out he and his mate were so loving and so capable. Now, I plunged into despair. The Niques had managed to separate my humans from me again. Could it be that even now, after I had bonded with my new human, they would steal him away from me? I listened in anguish.

"Mr. and Mrs. Kelley?"

"Yes?"

"We wanted you to be present when we drew the winner of the raffle."

"What raffle?"

"The raffle that you and all these other folks entered, to win the chihuahua!"

"What?"

"We're raffling off the chihuahua. There were too many people who wanted him, so we are letting luck decide who gets to take him home."

"Oh!"

My humans started laughing.

"Is that why there were so many forms?"

"Mmmhmm, we have to explain the lottery process and make it all legal."

"Wow, well, we don't want a chihuahua."

Whew!

Thank Kax!

That is twice now, that my humans have escaped the Niques' dirty little scheme to get them to adopt one of them instead of one of us Kaxians!

"You don't want the chihuahua?"

"No!"

"No."

Another pound employee got involved and tried to explain.

"These folks are adopting a dog from the big dog room."

And then one of the humans waiting for the results of the chihuahua raffle said the words I will remember and resent for the rest of my dog lives.

"If I don't get the chihuahua, I'm going to look in the puppy room."

That made my human say the only words I have ever heard that made me hurt all the way deep down inside me, where my eternal re-birthing consciousness abides.

"There's a puppy room? I didn't get to see the puppy room..."

He sounded like he was choking when he said it, with an ache in his voice, with yearning.

All my muscles turned to mush. I fell to the concrete floor of the clinic. I wanted to melt into the drain; I felt so small and unwanted. I howled. It was immature, but I couldn't help it.

"Hoooooooooooowwwl!"

He doesn't want me.

We bonded. I felt it. He's my human, and he doesn't want me. Of course not.

He's like all the rest of them. My parents' human didn't want me, so why should he. Randy didn't really want me. Why would this human be any different?

He wants a little puppy who is six weeks old and walks on wobbly legs and is much cuter than a six-month-old who is just about a dog already. That's what every human wants: a little, cute, clumsy, playful puppy who the human can mold into the desired pet.

Humans want little puppies who they can train just how they want, not old dogs they think can't learn new tricks.

Human!

Come back to me!

I'll do everything you say.

I can learn new tricks, and new commands.

I'm already your best friend.

I feel the dog bond with you.

I will be loyal, faithful, and true.

I already love you more than I love myself.

Don't you feel the dog bond?

I was sure you loved me, too.

The mate of the man I thought of as my human asked him if he wanted to go look in the puppy room.

"Do you want to go see it?"

Did I detect a note of sadness in her voice? A tiny kernel of hope erupted in my broken heart when he didn't answer right away. Hope grew as he hesitated for almost a minute.

"No, we already have our dog."

I needn't have worried over my new human being trapped by any of the Niques' schemes. Happy as I was to have my hope of the dog bond holding true on both ends fulfilled, he said something next that made me breathe a huge sigh of relief:

"And his name is Raffle!"

***

Neya shook herself.

Something inside her had changed. She sat in confusion for a moment, trying to figure out what was different. After a while, she gave up and focused once more on her mother's last tale to the wolf pups, before they would be in her care and she would be the one telling the tales.

"A long time ago, before anyone was born whose name we know, big stars fell out of the sky by the hundreds, and landed on the ground."

"And they didn't catch the forest on fire."

"And they were quiet, right Momma?"

"Right, my smart babies. The big stars landed on the ground without any noise at all. They were being driven here, in the way that humans drive cars and trucks on their roads."

"We are not to cross the roads!"

"The humans might smash us with their cars and trucks!"

"But no humans drove the big stars."

"Right, right, right!"

Fleek licked each eager young pup.

"No humans were driving the big stars, and they landed on the ground silently. We wolves gathered far away to watch. The big stars smelled like metal because they were made of metal. They opened up."

"And dog aliens came out!"

"They look like wolves!"

"They walk and talk like wolves!"

"But they are not wolves!"

"What good listeners you are! Yes, the dog aliens look like us and even walk and talk like us, but they came from the stars long before anyone whose name we know was born. All dog aliens look at least a little like wolves. Some are bigger than us..."

"Some are smaller!"

"Some have odd shapes!"

"Some of their ears hang down!"

"Right, right, right!"

Fleek licked all the pups again.

"The biggest difference between wolves and dog aliens is they don't all blend in with the desert. Some do, but you can see most of them from miles away. Almost all dog aliens smell like humans, and that is the easiest way to tell that you are dealing with a dog alien and not a wolf."

"And we might see them."

"But we don't trust them."

"The dog aliens are not our friends."

"No, the dog aliens are not our friends. They live with humans, as their pets. That is the easiest way to know it is a dog alien coming, when you smell one. They smell like humans."

"And they are not of our world!"

"Earth is not their mother!"

"The moon is not their father!"

"You have all started learning this story very well. I hope you listen to Neya as you have listened to me. From now on, she will be teaching you, while I resume my duties as alpha female of the pack."

Fleek looked over and backed up so that Neya could take her place.

Neya happily took her new place with the

pups. She vaguely remembered dreading this duty, but for the life of her, she couldn't remember why. It was very important for them to know these stories. They might keep the pups from making grave mistakes in judgment some day. She shrugged off her feeling of confusion and continued their education.

"Right, right, right! We don't trust the dog aliens because they are not of our world. Earth is not their mother, the way she is our mother. The moon does not rule them the way he rules us, as our father."

Neya licked each pup on the nose. She examined the look on each little wolf-pup face, to check for understanding before she finished the story in the traditional way.

"Dogs are aliens.
They are not our friends.
We don't trust the dog aliens."
***

Lido and Skil were running the vinyard that night when Blackie ran up and tackled Skil.

"Haha! You didn't see me coming!"

Blackie nipped at Skil playfully, the way Lido had been doing, and tried to roll over and over with her, as Lido had been doing.

Lido didn't know what to do. Blackie wasn't hurting Skil, but Lido sure didn't like seeing him play with her. It made him mad and sad all at once.

Skil didn't know what to do, either. She didn't particularly want to play with Blackie. She would rather be running with Lido. She wriggled out from under Blackie and ran back over to Lido.

Blackie tried to keep playing with Skil.

Lido had enough.

"Leave her alone! She's not playing."

"Are you gonna make me, Fatty?"

Every bit of Lido wanted to make Blackie leave Skil alone. But Blackie was the son of Boss, and Boss was going to decide if Lido mined with Skil or stayed here and ran the vinyard, with Blackie. Boss had to send him to the mine. Anything else would be unbearable. But, Skil had to want him to mine with her. Falling out of favor with Skil would be unbearable, too.

"Yeah, if I have to I'll make you."

Lido bared his fangs at Blackie and waited for the attack.

Skil wasn't going to stand by and let her friend be picked on, though.

"We'll both make you!"

Skil bared her fangs at Blackie, too.

"Aw, I see how it is. You like the fatty! OK, you go off with him, then. You're not good enough for me, anyway. The pack leader's son deserves a strong she..."

Blackie kept muttering to himself as he sauntered off.

Lido was embarrassed by what Blackie had said, because Skil had heard it. Sure, he wanted Skil to be his mate some day, when they were old enough, but right now he just wanted to play with her. Well, and he wanted to be the only male she played with.

Skil was thrilled that Lido had taken a stand for her, and relieved that he hadn't been hurt.

"Thank Kax you're all right!"

"Are you all right, Skil? Did he hurt you?"

"I'm fine. He nipped me, that's all. It was really brave of you to volunteer to make him leave me alone, Lido."

"I had to, Skil. I don't know what I would do if anything happened to you. You're all I ever think about."

"I didn't dare think about you as much as I wanted to, Lido, before you came to live here. But now that you're here, I am happier than I have ever been in my whole life!"

They finished their watch running the vinyard together, and playing sometimes. The next morning, Boss announced that Lido would be going to the mine with Skil. The two of them ran around in small circles with their tails wagging as fast as they could, they were so happy.

"Race ya to the mine!"

"Let's go!"

Blackie thought Boss seemed pleased with himself for sending them, too, sitting there on his haunches, watching them run off.

CHAPTER 11: DEN

My humans walked me out of the pound on a leash. I went with them joyfully. All my Kaxian buddies congratulated me and wished me well as I left. I nodded in response to them, but I didn't say anything, for fear of upsetting my humans. They put me behind the seat of their little pick-up truck, and drove me to my new den. Our home was a modest ranch-style house with yellow stucco on the outside, and it stood at the end of a dead-end street, on a cul de sac. There were many other houses on the street, and they were close together.

We went through a tall wooden gate into the fenced back yard. It was big enough for me to run in, but just barely. I would have to run in circles. Still, that beat running up and down the hall of a tiny apartment. Out of habit, I looked for holes under the fence. I didn't see any, but I saw places I might dig some. Instantly, I felt horror at the thought of leaving my bonded human, even for a day, against his wishes.

"Go potty, Raffle!"

But I had gone before we left the pound so as not to have to go inside their vehicle! Upset at not being able to obey their command, I jumped up and gave them hugs, instead.

"No! Down, Raffle!"

All right, they don't like hugs. I ran around the back yard with my tail high up in the air, to show that I loved my new home. I did! This grassy yard was far better than a kennel at the pound.

The man found a ball.

"Here Raffle!"

I came over and looked at the ball intently, to show that I knew he wanted me to fetch it.

"Get it, Raffle!"

I raced over and fetched the ball, then brought it back to the man.

His mate was impressed.

"Wow! Someone must have been training him! He already knows how to fetch!"

"Yeah! He's a good boy!"

I loved hearing that phrase, Good Boy. This was the first time I had heard it in this dog life. It had power over me, and the man knew it, but he was kind, so that was going to be OK.

Just then, I heard some snarling from the yard next to ours, on the other side of a tall wooden fence.

"Ha! Clem! So you've taken up residence there, eh? Well, you stay on your side of the fence, and no one will get hurt."

His voice triggered my Kaxian memories. Oh no! Fidetz was one of the most mean-spirited Niques I had ever met, and now he was my neighbor! From the pitch of his bark, he was a chihuahua in this dog life.

His humans had also adopted a Kaxian, though, a pit bull terrier named Regs.

"Don't worry, Clem, I got your back."

"Hah, easy for him to say, Clem, but you know he can't do much against me with us having the same humans."

"The name's Raffle, and oooh! Just try me, you little..."

"Help! Help! The big dog is attacking me!"

"Haha! Our humans are inside and can't hear you."

I was bent toward the ground as far from their yard as I could get, so that their arguing voices wouldn't hurt my ears. At the same time, I was listening to what they said. I needed to glean all the information I could in order to help me deal with my new Nique neighbor. I hoped my fellow Kaxian being there would somewhat mitigate the situation.

"Come, Raffle! Let's go inside."

Oh well, it looked like I was going inside my new humans' home. That was even better than being in the back yard. There was plenty of time to learn about my new neighbors, and I was sure I would.

We went through a sliding glass door into a large bedroom. The carpet was beige and the walls were white, but unlike Randy's apartment, this house felt lived in. Pictures hung on the walls. The shelves and ledges were full of mementos. Odds and ends such as sports equipment, craft items, gift-wrapping supplies, and the evidence of other hobbies filled every nook and cranny.

"Honey? Oh, there you are. I'm bringing Raffle inside, even though he hasn't peed yet. There are two dogs next door barking at him, and it's freaking him out."

"Oh, OK. Raffle! Want to see your dishes and your toys and your bed?"

"Do I!"

She laughed and showed me my sleeping crate by their bed, and then led me down the hall toward the kitchen.

I was distracted by the distinct smell of the cat who obviously lived here. Aha, I spotted the cat hiding under the couch, where it hissed at me. Cats are very intelligent Earth creatures. They can spot a non-Earth creature instantly. Good thing for us, they aren't very good at communicating with humans. They do try, though, which is why we often chase them off. I have been friends with many cats over my 99 dog lives, but this particular cat didn't seem very friendly at all toward dogs. She didn't even come out to sniff, just stayed there under the couch, hissing and growling at me. Her loss.

My humans showed me where my dishes were next. There was food in my food dish and water in my water dish. I guess she wanted to make sure I knew it was mine.

"Drink water, Raffle!"

That was an odd command, but I complied.

"Wow! Did you see that, Scott?"

"What?"

"I just told Raffle to drink some water, just as if I were talking to a kid, and he did it!"

"Really? Let me try. Raffle! Drink some water, Boy."

I wasn't really thirsty, but the dog bond compels me to obey, so I did.

"Good boy!"

I really love it when he says 'Good Boy!' I got all mushy inside and rolled over on my back. He petted and scratched my belly for a minute, and then went to get some toys they had bought for me.

"Look at this, Raffle! This is for you to chew up. See? Here you go!"

I contented myself with chewing on one of the stuffed toys and appealing very faintly to the cat for the next few hours while my humans watched TV. And then all that water they had made me drink caught up with me. I needed to go outside, immediately.

"I need to go outside! Could you let me out, please? It's urgent!"

"Quiet, Raffle!"

My human's mate surprised me with another new command.

Yet another surprise was that the dog bond now extended to her. I had to obey her command. I could no longer use my voice to try and get them to let me outside. I licked at their hands, but that just got them to pet me, so then I ran back and forth in front of the TV. That was a big mistake.

"Lie down!"

They both said that at the same time, as if they had rehearsed it. They looked at each other and giggled, and then settled back on the couch to finish watching their TV show. They were really very cute, holding hands.

As for me, well, you know what happened. When you've got to go, you've got to go. I held it for as long as I could, praying to Kax that my humans would release me from any of the commands preventing me from begging to go outside: lie down, quiet, down. I lost my battle with my bladder, though. Right there on the carpet in the living room, I emptied it.

"No!"

They both shouted when they heard my bladder emptying. This time, they didn't giggle. They were mad.

They hadn't given me a choice!

The cat glinted her eyes at me from under the couch, gloating at my ruination. She finally seemed happy now, which she hadn't been since I set foot in her home. She stretched out her paws slowly, one by one, making a show of cleaning herself. And then she walked right by me with her head held high and her tail straight up with the top tipped over to the side.

I liked these humans, too.

I had bonded with them, which would make being dropped off at the pound by them much more hurtful than it had been the last time, when my human hadn't even liked dogs. This time, I hoped I would not be adopted. The dog bond is so strong that it would be easier to just start over again as a new pup than it would be to live apart from the humans that had bonded with me.

Unreleased from any of the commands they had given me, I just had to lie there in the puddle that I had made. I couldn't help groaning a little as I waited for them to pack me off to the pound. OK, I made the crying sounds, too. I was miserable.

And then my human's mate surprised me again.

"Oh no, Scott! This is our fault!"

"What do you mean?"

"He tried to tell us he needed to go outside, but we told him to be quiet, and then we told him to lie down!"

Smart humans who love you are hard to find,

but I have two of the best on Earth.

CHAPTER 12: LIDO

That night in my new den, when I was almost asleep in my new crate by my new humans' bed, I prayed to Kax.

"Thank you for my new home. I am happy. I know I owe this to you, and that my first duty is to you and to my fellow Kaxians. I don't want to disobey my new humans to leave and go mine jex, though. They have not commanded me to remain at home, but I know they want it. I love them. I don't want them to abandon me. Please don't make me disobey them. Please. I'll do anything else you want, just let me stay here."

I didn't hear any answer, but a few hours later I woke up because Lido was just outside the window, whispering over and over.

"Clem! Clem! Clem! Wake up!"

I went over to the window, nosed the curtain aside, and looked out at him.

"Lido! It's great to see you! How's Skil?"

Lido grinned bigger than I ever saw him grin before. He stood up straighter, too, and sucked in his gut, which looked smaller, come to think of it. His chest even puffed out.

"She's great, Clem. I've already asked her to

be my mate, when we're old enough."

Wow! He didn't waste any time! I tried to hide my surprise by telling him my own news.

"Congratulations, Lido, that's great. Wow. That's good to hear. Huh. Hey, Well, you'll never guess what happened to me, so I'll just tell you: I've bonded with my new humans! I go by the name Raffle now."

Lido's eyes got big.

"Wow! You bonded with your humans?"

"Yep!"

"But you're only six months old!"

"I know!"

"What's it like?"

"It's wonderful and weird and kind of scary, Lido. It gives my humans control over me."

"What?"

Lido's eyes almost popped out of their sockets, and he jumped a little.

"Yeah, that's the 'kind of scary' part."

"It sounds more than just 'kind of scary,' Clem! Are you sure you're OK? I can probably get you out of there if..."

"Call me Raffle, Lido, and I know you could get me out, but I don't want to leave. I have to obey my new humans, but I love them, and they love me, so I don't mind at all. I like it. I want to please them, and I know they want what is best for me."

"Well, I guess what Heg said makes more sense now. He said you won't be mining with us anymore. He sent me here to tell you not to worry about coming to the mine, that you'll have shut-in duties from now on."

"That's a relief. My only worry has been how

on Earth I would fulfill my Kaxian duty without disobeying my new master."

At that last word, Lido took a big breath like he was going to launch into a speech, and then he seemed to change his mind.

"Heg also said to tell you, 'Sweet dreams.' What does that mean, Cle... I mean Raffle?"

I smiled at what Lido had said. Heh, so Heg would be showing me my new duties while I slept. I couldn't tell Lido that, though. It pained me to keep things from my best friend, but I had the feeling that even if I wanted to tell Lido, Heg's suggestion would prevent me.

"I can't tell you, Lido."

Lido started to say something, but then he just swallowed. His ears drooped, and his mouth slackened. His tail drooped, too.

"I would tell you if I could. You know that."

Lido shrugged.

"Well, I guess I better get back home."

"Say hi to Skil for me!"

I'm sure he heard me, but he just turned around and ran off.

I watched until he was out of sight, and then out of habit, I listened until he was out of earshot.

"Have a safe trip home, Lido."

I was talking to the empty window. At least he had Skil. I hoped they would be happy.

***

When I fell asleep that night, I told myself to watch in my dreams for a mental movie from Heg. Sure enough, I woke up with the memory that Heg had shared: me listening for messages tagged with my new name, Raffle, and relaying them on so that someone across town could hear from someone else who was out of earshot.

That was pretty simple.

Why couldn't Heg have just told Lido to tell me that? Why had he told Lido to tell me 'sweet dreams?' Why the mental movie and all the secrecy that entailed? I felt awful for having to keep the mental movies a secret from Lido.

Didn't Heg know that?

***

The next few days were wonderful despite my hurt feelings when Lido ran off and my bitterness at Heg for making me keep secrets from Lido. My new humans liked to play, and I was a puppy! Puppies are made for play. My new humans had bought me so many toys that I couldn't go ten feet without encountering one.

There were stuffed animals with little squeaky bulbs inside that were fun to tear out. In hindsight, I made quite a mess with the stuffing while tearing these apart, but my humans took it in stride, Kax bless them.

There were rubber toys that were particularly good for cutting my incoming teeth out of my gums. One in particular my humans would stuff with a treat and then hand to me to get the treat out. They seemed disappointed when I was able to get the treat out in five seconds, flat. I'll bet they wish to this day that they had shown me those teething toys before I made the tooth marks on the leg of the coffee table. I get embarrassed whenever a guest notices that, to this day.

There were balls: tennis balls, ping pong balls, and even a soccer ball. The cat was territorial over the ping pong balls. She chased them all under the dresser and the rocking chair, where only my nose could fit. I liked the tennis balls the best. They were fun to chew up into little tiny pieces. My humans enjoyed playing out in the back yard with me and the soccer ball. They would try to get the soccer ball to one side of the yard, and I understood it was up to me to stop them. They got tired really quickly when we played this, for some reason, so we only played for a few minutes at a time, but it was fun.

My human's mate's favorite of all my toys was a hard canvas cube with geometric holes in it that had plastic pieces which fit inside the cube through holes with corresponding geometric shapes. She was enthralled every time I solved the puzzle, which I found funny because it was super easy. It soon became my favorite toy, too. I would bring it to her whenever I wanted to see that funny look on her face.

My favorite game to play with her, though, was tug of war. She would take me outside and show me a cloth rope. I would grab the knotted end with my teeth and clamp on as hard as I could. She would swing the rope around, trying to unloose me. At first, she only made me run around her, but she got more and more daring until she was swinging me around and around her with my feet off the ground by a good bit, hanging on only by my teeth. I was only half grown then, only 35 pounds. That would never work now that I am 70 pounds (and my teeth are much older).

***

I waited for my female human to go off to work so that I could do my Kaxian relay duty without making her worry about what I was up to, but she never did. Instead, she went into a room in the house that she called her office, where she talked on the phone a lot about car crashes and injuries. She also typed a bunch on a laptop computer.

All this time, my male human was sleeping. He slept all day while my female human and I played and she talked on the phone in her office and the cat hissed at me from her cubbyhole in the bookshelf. I found this puzzling. Why did he sleep all day? I found out that night. He left for work after it got dark!

After my male human left for work, my female human had more play time with me, and ate her meal, and talked on the phone about much more pleasant things than car accidents and injuries, and watched the TV, and played games on the computer out in the living room.

Between my two humans, one working days and the other working nights, I was never alone in the house. (Well, the cat was always there, too, but what could she do?)

On one level, constant human affection was wonderful, especially after being abandoned by my first human and almost abused by my second human. Here in my third human home, I never felt lonely. I basked in all the love and attention and play time they gave me. I felt real love, and I loved them back.

On another level, my Kaxian level to be precise, constant human company worried me. It limited me, to be more precise. Sure, I could always listen for messages tagged with my name and relay them. Relaying messages bothered whichever of my humans was sleeping, but I was always careful to face a window or a door when I did so, to make them think an intruder was passing by. I was relaying messages and would continue.

Wait.

One time, there actually was an intruder.

It was the middle of the night. My male human was at work, and my female human was sleeping. I was shut up in my sleeping crate by their bed. I heard a human opening the window in the front of the house! I yelled and yelled about the intruder until my female human woke up. She had the sense to let me out of the crate, and I ran to the front window and told the girl who was crawling in the window that she had better not or I was going to eat her for...

Yes! A teenaged human girl was trying to crawl in through the front window of my humans' home. We found out later from the neighbors that the house we rented used to be inhabited by drug dealers and had people crawling into it from windows at all hours of the day and night, and they even had carrier pigeons in a coop on the roof, for the drug business, so craziness was actually commonplace to the neighbors. My humans thanked me profusely for keeping intruders out from then on, so the location actually was prime for being a shut-in who had to pretend to warn off intruders while really relaying messages.

But, relaying messages didn't seem like the kind of thing that would get me promoted. I had all sorts of questions, and no one here to ask.

How did any Kaxian who was bonded to a human (or any Nique who was bonded to a human, for that matter, but who cared about them?) manage to get promoted?

How did they manage to serve Kax?

What had my dad meant when he said he served a higher purpose as a bonded dog than mining for jex?

Wasn't mining our purpose here on Earth?

Didn't jex have to be our priority?

Had Heg given up on me?

All in all, though, I was happy. I had a better home than I ever hoped for, with humans who cared about me and played with me and arranged their schedules so that I wouldn't be lonely. Not many Kaxians ever get that much consideration from humans. I knew that Kax had blessed me, so I tried to just be grateful.

Not every day over the next six months was as uneventful as these first few days, though.

CHAPTER 13: CAT

Did I mention that my master's mate's cat did not like me, at all? That she hissed whenever I came near her? That practically all I ever saw of her were her glowing eyes under the bed or the couch or the bookcase? That she wished I would drop dead and wouldn't hesitate to speed the act along if she thought she could get away with it? That doesn't even begin to cover how horrible it was for us to live together.

To be fair, I was the new addition to the family, an imposter. From our female human's phone conversations, I knew the cat had been with our mistress for years before our two humans met, let alone married. The cat had a far longer claim on the humans than I had. Still, I did not in any way deserve all the bitterness the cat showed me or the mean ways she never passed up an opportunity to tell me what an awful interloper she thought I was.

All right, the cat had a name.

The humans called her Puritan.

Unusual, huh?

The cat was a black and white domestic short-hair. She looked like the pilgrims that children draw for Thanksgiving, if that helps you picture her.

Well, OK, she didn't have buckles on her feet or wear a hat, Silly. She had white feet, a black back, and a white stomach. She reminded my mistress of the puritans at the renaissance fair where she used to work, and where she had adopted the cat, and where she got her name.

Puritan had been the runt of her litter. Her mother's humans had been performers who traveled from fair to fair by car. They would stop at campgrounds along the way, where they would let the cats out to do their business and to hunt. When they pulled out of one such stop, no one in the troop had noticed that the mom cat was not in the car. By the time they were at the next stop and missed the mom cat, it was too late to turn back and get her. The troop would have been late for their next gig.

The mom cat had been left behind when the kittens were only four weeks old. The humans fed them cat food, but they were barely able to digest it yet. This stunted Puritan's growth for life, so she was small for her fifteen years of age. Humans often mistook her for a kitten and were surprised at how grumpy she was.

With anyone but our mistress, Puritan would tolerate petting or playing for exactly ten seconds, and then she would bite. Our master was always fooled by the cat's tail. He thought she was happy with him petting her, because her tail was "wagging." He was always surprised when she turned and bit the hand that was petting her.

Here's a word to the wise:

Cats do not wag their tails when they are happy, the way dogs do. When a cat is happy, her tail will be straight up, with just an inch or so at the top tipped sideways. If a cat's tail is moving, the cat is either angry or hunting. A hunting cat's tail will slither like a snake. An angry cat's tail will thump the floor like a jump-rope. Mistake this for wagging her tail at your peril! When a cat is angry or hunting, she is likely to claw or bite.

Puritan knew I was from out of this world.

This had to be frustrating for her.

She tried and tried to tell her mistress, but humans don't understand cats very well. Kaxians don't understand cats very well, either (and neither do Niques, but who cares about them?). Every time Puritan would try to tell her mistress I was an alien, it would be my duty to chase her off. I felt bad for it, but duty is duty. My memories told me it wasn't always this way between Kaxians and cats, but usually we had to meet when we were both young, if we were going to be friends.

You probably are thinking my power of suggestion should have helped me deal with the cat better. Well, let me tell you, it was of no help at all.

Reaching out to to a human's mind is almost as effortless for me as reaching out to a fellow Kaxian's mind. We think alike, you humans and we Kaxians (and Niques, but who cares about them?). We're both civilized. Even though cats are Earth creatures and I am the imposter, it seems like the cats are the ones from another planet.

A cat's mind is alien to me: completely wild. You humans only think you have cats tamed. In reality, they have you tamed. You feed them, give them water, treat them for disease, and keep the rain and snow off their backs. What do cats do for you? OK, some cats are good mousers. Admit it, though:

most cats do nothing at all for their keep, and are so independent minded that their humans can't even get them to come when called.

When Puritan was asleep, my power of suggestion was blocked by her mind being full of the excitement brought on by her vivid dreams. She dreamed constantly of hunting and killing things. Cats are little killing machines. It's a wonder humans let them inside their houses at all, but it's especially frightening that cats prowl about human homes while the humans are sleeping!

No, I could not see her dreams. I could tell what she was dreaming by her phantom dream movements. If you don't know what I mean, watch an animal sometime while it is sleeping. Its paws will move as if it is running, or hunting. Really.

Puritan was lazy, too. OK, she was old. I was the one who had to keep the rodents out of the house. All she ever did was eat, sleep, hiss at me, torment me, and sometimes play with our mistress.

When Puritan was awake, her mind was too full of hatred for me to allow any suggestions to get in. Whenever I got near the cat, she made this high-pitched growling sound, deep in her throat. It sounded like someone was revving up a remote-controlled car, but not fun like that. She meant it as a warning that she was about to attack me. I'm sure she would have killed me in my sleep if my humans hadn't given me the safety of a sleeping crate.

***

Whenever I ate, I was careful to make sure my humans were nearby. This was mostly out of my fear of being abandoned again, but it was also because the cat loved to attack me while I ate. I had the habit of wagging my tail when I ate. The humans thought this was cute, and really, it was my way of expressing my happiness.

Well, the cat just loved to run up and bite or claw my tail as it wagged. And, the humans thought that was cute, too! I wasn't sure what to make of this.

I tried and tried to hold my tail still while I ate, but sooner or later I would get so wrapped up in how good the food tasted that I would forget. The second my tail started wagging, out popped the cat. She would be hiding nearby, always someplace different. With one pounce, she would be on my tail, either biting it or clawing it. It didn't really harm me, but it sure was a mean way to disturb my meal.

***

I thought of a way to fight back.

Our humans tolerated her attacks as just silliness because she wasn't really hurting me, just disturbing me. OK. Turnabout is fair play.

The next time Puritan was settled in our mistress's lap getting petted, I made my move. I sidled up to the front of the couch where I could reach the cat with my mouth, and I proceeded to give her a bath.

You would have thought I was poking her with a fork, the way she growled!

"GGGGgggggggggRRRRRRllllllllll!"

Our female human laughed so hard her face turned red.

I got done washing Puritan's back, and proceeded to wash her face.

"MMmmmmmmmmRRRRRRRllllllll!"

She growled at a completely new level, letting me know she was not happy at all with the attention and love I was showing her.

I could tell the cat wanted to claw something, but our mistress was all she would hurt if she did, so the cat was stuck.

Puritan had to sit there and be nice while I washed her.

I washed her ears for her, just to show how considerate I was. Next, I washed her paws.

She reflexively extended her claws so that I could clean between her toes, but she did not claw me once. She just kept growling, one note higher and more sustained than the last.

"BBbbbbbrrrrrraaaaaawwwwwwllllllll!"

***

The cat got back at me in such a way that got her relegated permanently to the bathroom. She spent the rest of her days there. Don't feel too bad for her. It was a huge 12 x 12 bathroom, as big as a small bedroom. She had her bed in there, and her food and water were up high on a counter-top, far away from her litter box on the floor.

Still, I wonder if she thought this consequence was worth her worst attack on me, which happened right in front of our mistress.

Our master often brought home things he had found in the street or near the dumpsters of apartment complexes at the end of the month: furniture, clothing, toys, books, and even tools. One day it was a bench for the yard. Another time it was a bird feeder. Twice he brought home functional, expensive exercise equipment which other humans had abandoned because they were too lazy to move it. Often, he brought home toys for me. My master's mate would wash whatever it was and then find a place for it in our home. It was nice, how he provided for us.

One time, my master brought home a child's sleeping bag that he thought I could use as a bed in the room that our mistress used as an office. So, I made my daytime bed on this cute little pink princess sleeping bag. Don't laugh! It was nice and comfortable, and I appreciated the gesture.

Puritan did not like this at all, for two reasons. Number one, she didn't want to share our mistress. She was possessive. Number two, she never got presents from our master. This was his fault, that he showed blatant favoritism to me, but she took it out on me. Lucky me.

This cat was fifteen years old.

She was housebroken.

Or, in human terms, she was potty trained.

But, **she peed on my sleeping bag!**

She did it to show her contempt for me, and for no other reason.

I had gotten up off my bed briefly, perhaps to go get a drink of water or something. I was in the hallway when I heard the sound of the cat peeing. I smelled it then, too, and rushed back into the little office.

Our poor mistress was on a corded phone, talking with one of her insurance claimants, discussing a serious injury. She couldn't react to what the mean old cat was doing in a way that the caller could hear, and her phone cord "leash" wouldn't let her go far from her desk, but Kax bless her, she sure did let the cat have it with her foot!

That darn cat was determined, though! She maneuvered around my sleeping bag to where our mistress couldn't get to her, and continued to pee on my little sleeping bag!

Equally determined, our mistress grabbed the corner of the sleeping bag and pulled it out from under the cat.

The cat fell undaintily onto her bottom.

Now, our mistress was still on the phone, and she needed to be typing notes on her laptop computer about the crucial information the insurance claimant was giving, but here she was, holding up a pee-soaked pink princess sleeping bag that was about to start dripping on the brown carpet.

"Can I call you back?"

CHAPTER 14: WORK

When I had been with my new master a few months, I had settled into a routine. My master would wake me up each morning with the sound of his truck coming home from work. The two of us would play fetch in the back yard for half an hour or so, and then he would feed me. I would lie at his feet while he watched TV for a few hours until he went to bed, and then I would go lie on my soiled but laundered pink princess sleeping bag in my mistress's office and listen to her business phone calls about car accidents and the injuries people claimed had resulted from these accidents. After she finished work, my master would wake up and we would all eat dinner, and then a few hours later it would be time for bed.

One evening, my mistress had an idea.

"Why don't you take Raffle to work with you tonight?"

"Uh, I guess that might be fun!"

Now, that sounded like fun to me, too, but I hadn't slept all day, as had my master. I was just winding down for bedtime when we left for work.

Working with Scott was fun! He was guarding a complex of freshly built, uninhabited human dens. Most of them were finished, but some were still being built. Our nightly duty was to walk into each den and make sure no one was living there. I tried to explain to him that I could smell there were no humans in the entire complex, but of course he didn't understand. We had to do our job the difficult, human way.

It was a bit creepy out there, even though my nose told me we were alone. These new dens were at the edge of civilization.

Before men came to live in Southern California, the place was a desert. This new housing tract butted right up on what is still the wild desert, complete with cactus and sage brush that turns into tumbleweeds. Coyotes have a very real presence out there, and every once in a while we could hear the eerie sound of coyotes yipping.

My master wasn't afraid. I admired his courage. He didn't even carry one of those gun weapons that many humans rely on. He only had a long flashlight that he carried the way a human carries a night stick. His movements were fluid at all times, and his steps were sure. I wasn't at all sure what to make of that vision I'd had of him fighting off people at the pound, but I was pretty confident he knew how to fight. I was also sure that my part in our partnership was to be the eyes, ears, and nose, as well as to help him fight if it came to that.

Secretly, I vowed to get him inside with the doors closed, if the coyotes ever came. I knew he would be OK in a fight with one or two humans, but those coyotes run in large packs.

Most of the time, the two of us were alone the whole night. All of that walking kept us in pretty good shape, so it wasn't a total waste.

But, that first night, I was falling asleep on my feet. Any time my master would stop for more than a minute, I would be out cold. Without even reaching out to his mind, I could tell he was getting frustrated.

The ninth or tenth time he pulled on my leash to wake me up, I heard some humans getting out of a vehicle on the other side of the complex we were guarding. I sprang to my feet and told him what I heard.

"Four humans just got out of a large van on the other side of the complex, Scott! Over this way!" I went as far in the direction of the intruders as I could, inside the room in the human den.

He couldn't understand me, of course, but he knew I was telling him we had company, and in which direction he could find the intruders.

"Good boy!"

I love it when he says that.

We got in his truck to drive over to the other side of the complex.

It was warm in the truck.

I fell asleep.

I woke up to Scott talking on his phone.

"Yes, they are loading property into their van! They are not authorized to take anything! Please come stop them before they get away!"

He ended the call on a grumpy note.

I sat up in the front seat of the truck and looked out the windshield.

A block away and around the corner from where we were parked, four men in dark clothing were each removing a window air conditioner from a different one of the new dens we were guarding.

Their van idled in the middle of the street. They were too far away for me to use my power of suggestion, but I thought Scott was smart to park far enough away that they couldn't see inside our vehicle. I wondered how we had arrived there without them noticing, but guessed lack of knowledge was what I got for sleeping on the job.

Trying to make up for that lost time I had been sleeping, my mind was working fast.

"Hm. I imagine Scott just called the police. It looks like these men are going to get away before the police arrive, unless we stop them."

Several fight scenarios played out in my head in the seconds it took me to decide what to do. My conclusion was that the four of them were spread out too far for the two of us to take them on in a fight. Besides, one of them had one of those gun weapons. I could smell gunpowder on him. Our only chance to stop them was for me to get close enough to use my power of suggestion.

Like I said, my mind was working overtime.

"Kax! What am I going to suggest to them?"

"I doubt I can make all four of them randomly decide that stealing is a bad idea. Could I make them fight each other? No, they are too far apart for that to make sense. In just another minute, they will have removed those air conditioners out of the windows. I need to suggest something that will make them all want to get into the human dens they are robbing, get behind another door, brace it, and stay there until the police arrive. I need to make them afraid. What can I make them fear, Kax?"

I didn't hear any answer from Kax, but I did get an idea. I would make them sort of afraid of... me.

I happened to know that my master kept the cab light in the truck turned off so that he could open his doors at night without calling attention to himself. I was proud of him. He had really thought things through.

I needed to get out of the truck if I was going to get close enough to those robbers to use my power of suggestion on them. I did not want him to come with me. He couldn't run as fast as I could. He was safer in the truck.

I looked at the door and whined to be let out. At the same time, I reached out to his mind and showed a mental movie of him opening the truck door and letting me out, and then me peeing in the sprouting grass along the brand new parking strip. I did this to protect him, so I did not have any qualms about using my power of suggestion on my master.

"OK, Puppy, make it quick."

He opened the door to the truck.

As soon as I was out of the truck, I put a picture in Scott's mind of him staying in the truck. I then ran toward the four men, talking as fast as I could and in different pitches, in order to make myself sound like a whole pack, instead of one.

"Look out!"

"The coyotes are coming!"

"You better run!"

"You better hide!"

"Lock yourself up safe inside!"

As soon as I was within range, I reached out to their minds, all four at once.

They were calm, cool, and collected, concentrating on their thievery like the professionals they were. Their minds were perfectly blue, and easy to reach. So, my suggestion took without resistance.

I circled around them while I continued my yipping and put in all their minds a mental movie of a pack of coyotes running in from the dessert, getting close enough to attack any second. I also placed in their minds the sounds of coyotes yipping, as I yipped, willing my suggested sound to be the one their brains told them they heard...

All four robbers scrambled into the empty human dens through the windows where they had removed air conditioners. They each went through the next door they found, closed it, braced it, and stood there trembling.

I continued the yipping suggestion and my own yipping until the police arrived, and then I ran back to my master's truck and sent a mental movie of him getting out and talking to the police.

And then I crawled back into the truck and fell fast asleep again.

CHAPTER 15: MISTER

My Nique neighbor, Mister the chihuahua, never passed up a chance to taunt me. Every time my humans let me out through the sliding glass door into the back yard to do my business (and they were now wonderful about noticing when I told them I needed to go outside), Mister would use his doggie door and go outside, too, where he would mouth off to me through the fence the entire time I was outside:

"Ooh, look, it's the big tough Clem, going now by the human name Raffle."

"Could you be any more domesticated?"

"I heard you're not even interested in leaving the yard anymore!"

"Haha! Clem's gone native!"

He never once let up.

I tried to reach out to Mister's mind and suggest that he knock it off, but his mind was so full of contempt that it was impenetrable, even while he was sleeping.

To make matters worse, my misguided humans thought the three of us dogs were all friends. More often than I liked (which would have been just once), they arranged "play dates" when the neighbor humans would come into our yard with their two dogs. It was expected that we all three would play together, so that is what we did. Remember what I told you was the foremost command from Kax? (It is from Nique, too, but who cares about that?)

No humans can know that dogs are aliens.

This command is serious business. If we break this command, we are not reborn.

The humans do think we are animals, though, and animals do fight, so sometimes I would let the wolf in me have its way and start to attack Mister.

"Ggggrrrrrruff!"

I'd growl, and bite at Mister's belly.

Regs would always stop me, though.

"Gggggrarff!"

He'd growl, too, and bite at my neck.

I would turn to face the threat, and the two of us would tumble off in a wrestle of mouths snapping at throats. Although we were about the same age, Regs' Pit Bull body was twice as heavy as my Australian Cow Dog / German Shepard body, and his jaws opened twice as wide. He always succeeded at getting me off the "brother" his human pack had given him.

Our humans would stand around laughing and saying:

"Look at them go!"

"Yeah, that is how they practice."

"And learn. They are teaching each other how to defend themselves."

"They sure do enjoy play fighting!"

We were only half playing. If I ever got the chance to actually kill Mister, I might just do it. Bad enough that his kind were jex thieves, but he was also the biggest jerk I had met so far in this life. He was worse than Millie's Snookems, and that is saying something.

Regs was my fellow Kaxian, but the dog bond overrode that. He was bonded to his humans, too, as I was. They expected Regs to defend his "brother," and so he obeyed them.

One day, we were having one of these "play dates" in the front yards of our houses and out into the cul de sac that we lived on. Regs and Mister's human was throwing one stick out into the cul de sac, and the three of us were competing to be the one to bring it back to him.

I could run the fastest, so I almost always got to the stick first. However, Regs' American Staffordshire terrier jaws were the strongest. If he managed to get hold of the stick before I got it back to the human, he almost always managed to get it out of my mouth. Sometimes, the stick would drop to the ground, and Mister would grab it and actually be the one to bring it back. The game was actually fun, and a good contest of our various abilities.

A message tagged for Raffle came right when the human threw the stick. I needed to listen carefully to the message and then relay it, so I couldn't run after the stick. I needed an excuse to stop playing the stick game and stay where I was.

"Kax! What now?"

I didn't hear any answer.

Ooh, but then I got an idea. I pretended to hear small prey in the bushes nearby. Perking up my ears to listen to the message, I turned toward the bushes to make it seem like I had heard something in there. I wagged my tail slightly to make myself seem wrapped up in hunting small prey in the bushes, and having fun.

I guess it worked, because everyone just went on playing the stick game without me. If they had been in my pack, they would have joined me, but Regs and Mister knew I wasn't going to share anything I caught with them. Mister and I were enemies, and Regs was in Mister's pack, so he was my enemy, too. Sad, but true.

I heard the message that was tagged for me.

"Gara needs Mlic."

How odd. One Kaxian needed another Kaxian's presence. I relayed the message right away, and then I puzzled over it for a few seconds, until I heard my master's truck coming home. When it rounded the corner onto our cul de sac, Mister's human took us all into their back yard.

"What was it?"

Regs was asking me.

Whoa! That's right, Regs understood the messages I was relaying. This was getting complicated.

"Oh, nothing."

I was hoping he would let it go.

"Heh, you didn't even come close to catching it, did you?"

Whew! He was speaking in the language that Mister could understand, and playing along with my hunting charade.

"I would have had it if your master hadn't called us back here just then."

"Heh! Sure you would have!"

"You couldn't kill a fly!"

What do you know, Mister was back to taunting me again, right on cue.

I lunged for Mister's belly.

Regs lunged for my neck.

I jumped straight up in the air, out of Regs' reach. He was right on me again when I landed, though, and we went tumbling across the yard, mouths open and snapping at each other's throats.

The human did nothing to stop us, because after all, this is why the humans brought us together: to "play."

We were half playing.

Thank Kax, that was when my master came into the neighbor's yard and took me home.

With friends like Mister, who needs enemies? Well, maybe I couldn't kill Mister, but I wasn't helpless. I had some power, and I was going to try using it to see if I could get Mister's doggie door sealed up. Let him have to beg to be let out! That should teach him some manners. That would be hard on Regs, too, but I wasn't thinking about him.

That night when Mister was digging out of his yard to go help his Nique pack steal some Kaxian jex, I reached out to his human's mind. His human was asleep, and that wouldn't do for my plan. No problem. At least I had learned something from my time with Randy. I suggested that Mister's sleeping human needed to wake up.

It worked. I could tell when the human awoke. His mind became more lucid. Freshly awakened, it was not full of any particular emotion, either, nice and calm and perfectly blue.

I sent Mister's human a mental movie of Mister digging under the fence.

In my mind's eye, I "saw" Mister's human's mind starting to fill with pink alarm, and then red anger.

Before it filled too full for my power of suggestion to reach inside, I sent a mental movie of Mister going through the doggie door to get to the fence, and then changed it to a picture of the doggie door boarded up. I zoomed in on the nails in the boards to make them really thick and strong. There. That ought to do it!

It didn't work out the way I had planned.

One morning when my master and I got home from work, Mister, Regs, and their humans had moved out. They left a bunch of furniture behind in their garage. My master went over and talked to the landlord (who also owned our house and happened to be a deputy to the sheriff).

"Is this furniture abandoned? Up for grabs?"

"Hello, Scott. I don't know that yet, but once I confirm it, you are more than welcome to take this stuff."

"What happened to him? Why did he leave so suddenly? I thought he liked it here."

"He called and insisted that I board up the doggie door, blaming it for all the holes his dog dug under the fence. I didn't take too well to the tone in his voice, let alone the fact Mister had dug under the fence. My patience was exceeded when he insisted I come right over and address the problem. He was far from reasonable, and in the end I asked him to leave."

"I gave him until the end of the month, but he hadn't paid his rent yet, and he still hasn't. I guess he figured it was cheaper to just leave right away. I am surprised that he left all this stuff behind. I don't have any forwarding address, so if the stuff is still here by the end of the month, you can take whatever you want."

To this day, my humans still have a dresser that smells like Mister. That is not the worst of it, by far. Let me tell you, I would have been better off never suggesting anything at all to Mister's human.

The older couple of humans who moved into Mister and Regs' house had TWO Nique dogs: a female chihuahua named Cherry and a male miniature poodle named Fred. With no Regs to keep them in line, they were even more obnoxious to me than Mister had been. Oh, and they were friends with Snookems, Millie's obnoxious little Pomeranian. They gave me "greetings" from him every day. As if I needed that.

On the plus side, no one thought the three of us were friends, and they were bonded to their humans, so they didn't dig out to go help steal Kaxian jex.

On the minus side, their female human liked me, so she volunteered to watch me on the rare days when both my humans left the house. Nice going, Raffle. Before, you at least had some chance of making a promotion, some time. Now, you are watched 24 hours a day, seven days a week, 365 days a year by humans who love you and who make sure you have all that you need and no excuse to go anywhere. Nice work.

Oh, and wait until you hear the new neighbor woman's nickname for me. It started out as 'Pumpkin', and that was bad enough. She shortened it, though. I was soon known to her as 'Punkie'. I guess that was better than 'Piggie', but not by much.

"Ooh! Hiya Punkie!"

This was how she greeted me whenever she saw me, no matter who could see or hear. Her voice went up about two octaves while she said it, so that by the time she got to the e sound at the end, she was shrieking. This didn't particularly hurt my ears, but it sure hurt my male pride. And then, she would pull at my cheeks the way old ladies pull at the cheeks of human babies!

The doggie door was still there and perfectly functional, too. Every time I went outside I heard it from TWO Niques then. Two Niques who were not only hateful, but jealous of the attention their human lavished on me.

"Ooh, the wittle momma's boy got let out!"

"Better hurry up!"

"Yeah, get it all out before your humans make you go back inside!"

You can bet I considered suggesting to the new humans that they seal the doggie door. I considered it every minute whenever I was outside. I wasn't going to be rash this time, though. I was going to learn a little more about the power of suggestion before I tried something new again.

I barked out a message to the Kaxian shut-in relay system:

"Raffle wants to speak with Heg."

And then, while I was curled up on my pink princess sleeping bag in my mistress's office, trying in vain to sleep, I got another bright idea. In order to implement it, I took stock of the possible targets of my new mental abilities.

On the "no way" side:

I couldn't get through to Puritan because she

was a predator, always excited about the prospect of hunting. I wasn't going to mess with the minds of the Niques' humans until I got further guidance. Messing with them once had backfired, and as the saying goes, "Once bitten, twice shy." I couldn't get into the Niques' minds. Even when they were sleeping, somehow they were filled with contempt for me, so that I couldn't get through to them. I wondered how Heg managed, and thought maybe his pictures slipped in easier than my movies.

On the "working so far" side:

I easily got into the mind of my master in order to protect his safety, but otherwise the idea repelled me. I was reasonably sure the same would apply to my mistress. At non-emotional moments, it was also easy to get into other humans' minds. It was just as easy to get into fellow Kaxians' minds.

But wasn't there a third side?

I had failed to get into a predator's mind. However, I hadn't yet tried to play any mental movies for prey animals. Could I use prey animals to get the Niques to stop pestering me, or at least to get the Niques on the defensive for once? I realize now that getting even was childish, but the temptation just proved way too strong!

Did I mention that our cat was so old that ever since I moved in, I had been the one keeping the mice out of the house? Well, I could see now that I had been going about this all wrong. Imagine! I had been using the wolf part of me to keep the mice out, by sheer physical intimidation.

What if I played mental movies for the mice, instead? What should I have the mice do instead of coming into our house? And mice weren't the only prey animals at my disposal.

I could smell many other possible targets of my scheming. There were moles out in the yard, under the grass. There were large rats in the ivy on the hill that ran down to the highway at the end of our cul de sac, on the other side of a chain link fence and a hedge. There were snakes there, too.

Extending my hind leg up to scratch my ear, I ruminated on what sort of mental movie I might play for the mice, the moles, the rats, or the snakes in order to get them to help me seek my revenge on my pesky Nique neighbors.

CHAPTER 16: HEG

Right about then is when the first strange message came in from Heg. It came in a dream, but I knew it was from Heg. It showed him sending the pack members over to me one at a time, and then it showed me using my power of suggestion on them with message he was about to give me:

"Remember to pray to Kax."

How weird!

That was my reaction, but I was not able to respond to Heg. It was a dream. I was sleeping. When I woke up, he was long gone.

From my experience with suggestion, I figured while Heg was still there, he would only have caught my sleeping reactions in the form of the emotions which his suggestions triggered in me: pink excitement and purple confusion.

Heg's pictures didn't make any sense to me. Why couldn't Heg suggest to all the pack members himself? Why send them to me? Why only send one at a time, and not all at the same time?

I knew I would be able to suggest to the whole pack at once, with no need of this "one at a time" plan. I didn't want to be insubordinate to Heg, so I kept these questions to myself.

Besides, this was exciting! I had a special mission to accomplish. Maybe I was being groomed for a promotion, after all. My heart filled with hope.

I was working nights, so when I got up it was usually the time of day when most of the pack were going to sleep. I figured I would have to wait until I got home the next morning before I got my first assignment. I was wrong. He came almost as soon as I was awake, and it was Lido.

"Hi, uh, Raffle."

"Hey Lido! Glad to hear from you. How's Skil?"

"She's fine. Thanks for asking. Hey, Heg says you're lonely here for us, so we each have to come see you. Today is my day to come. I want you to know I'm sorry for running off last time without saying goodbye or anything. If Heg told you stuff and said not to tell me, then you have to do what he says. It was not fair for me to get mad at you. I'm sorry. Will you forgive me?"

"Aw, of course I forgive you, Lido! Now stop being so down in the dumps! How are you going to cheer me up if you sound like someone ate your last dog biscuit?"

His spirits were lifting. The moment between his sadness at feeling sorry and his happiness at being forgiven was my chance. I reached out to Lido's mind and planted a little movie in his head, of him praying to Kax, per my assignment from Heg.

Lido paused for a long moment. His mind went from pale sad blue to purple confusion, instead of the pink happiness it had been headed toward.

"I just got the idea that I need to pray to Kax, uh, Raffle. You mind if I just go ahead and do that

138

now?"

"Of course not. Go on."

"Kax! Please don't be angry with my parents. They taught me to pray to you. They did. I know I don't pray as much as I should. Please forgive me. Your friend, Lido."

The tone of Lido's voice changed when he was speaking to me again.

"Well, uh, Raffle, I hope I did cheer you up a little, by coming by."

"Yeah! Lido, it was great to see you. I'm glad you stopped by. Please say 'Hi' to Skil for me."

"I'm pretty sure you can say 'Hi' to her, yourself. Heg will be sending everyone by to see you, Raffle, so you shouldn't feel so lonely. I'm glad I got to come on the first day."

"Yeah, I'm glad, too. Take care of yourself and of Skil, and I guess I'll see you next time."

"I guess so! Bye for now!"

"Bye for now, Lido."

We both were talking with smiles on our faces. Lido ran away this time with a much lighter step, even though he was as heavy as ever.

Skil did come by, the next evening.

"Hi, eh, Raffle!"

"Hi Skil! It's great to see you!"

I was looking at her through the window.

"How's everything? Are you and Lido getting along now that you both have the same humans?"

Skil swung her head toward the ground for a moment, and then peeked up at me, just with her eyes. The tip of her tail was wagging slightly.

"Yes, we have agreed to be a mated pair, once we're old enough."

"Oh, that's great, Skil! I am very happy for you. I wish you all the best."

I found my chance to give Skil the suggestion to pray to Kax in between her shyness and her elation at my congratulations.

Her prayer was sweet.

"Kax! Give us healthy pups!"

I went to work with my master each night, and then each morning or evening a different pack member would come by to see me. We would make small talk, and I would manipulate the conversation so that they would have a moment of neutral emotions, which gave me the chance to insert the assigned suggestion that they pray to Kax. Some of them prayed out loud, as Lido and Skil had done. Most of them just got quiet for a few seconds, and prayed silently, inside their heads. They all took my suggestion and acted on it, though. I felt good about that, successful.

I understood that Heg had told the pack members I was lonely as an excuse to send them to me, but now I realized it was true. I was lonely for the pack, and I was glad to hear each member's voice.

Heg returned the day after the last pack member had come to visit me. My master was sleeping. My mistress was in her office, talking on the phone and typing on her laptop computer. Puritan was in the huge bathroom, where she always was nowadays. I went to talk to Heg at the sliding glass door in the living room. He jumped over the low stone wall around the patio and met me on the other side of the glass, wagging his tail.

"You did well, Raffle! Your power of suggestion is strong, and you are progressing well with your training."

This made me feel all puffed up, like my body was now bigger than it had been before he spoke. I was impatient.

"What exactly am I training to be, Heg?"

His tail stopped wagging. He paced back and forth a few times, looking at the floor. Finally, he sighed.

"That is something you need to ask Kax."

"Kax never answers me. How will I know what the answer is, if I just ask Kax?"

"When the answer comes, you will know."

We both sat quietly while I thought about that for a while. Now that I had asked my most secret and urgent question, I became brave and figured I might as well ask all the other questions that had been pestering me lately.

"Heg?"

"Yeah?"

"My parents never left the yard with me to mine jex. Not once. I didn't hear them relaying any messages for the pack, either. What Kaxian duty do my parents do?"

Heg sat down and looked at me sideways, with his ears tipped down.

"Did they teach you to pray to Kax?"

"Yeah, but..."

"Do you?"

"Yeah, I do, but..."

"Then your parents are doing their duty, which is to make sure all their pups know this place is not our home, that they are Kaxians and not dogs born of Earth."

"It seems like we could mine and guard much

more jex, though, if all the adult Kaxians mined or guarded, too. Isn't mining jex the reason we are here on Earth?"

"It is. But what would the humans think, if every dog on Earth were mining jex every day?"

"I get it. If every Kaxian (and every Nique, too, but who cares about them?) were mining all the time, then the humans would wonder why. They would investigate. They might realize that we are space aliens, and not dogs born of Earth."

"Yep."

"But Heg, this life, my body has been altered. The pound did that. I won't be able to have pups to raise up to know they are Kaxians."

"You are helping me raise the pack's pups, Raffle. Your power of suggestion is strong, and it is helping them remember their duty is first to Kax, unless and until they bond with humans."

"That's another question I have, Heg. Why do we Kaxians allow the dog bond?"

"Do you dislike the dog bond?"

"No! The dog bond is wonderful. I am so happy with my master and mistress, but it severely limits the Kaxian duty I can do."

"Oh, you're wrong, there. You bonded extremely young, Raffle. That means your power of suggestion is strong."

I raised one eyebrow.

Heg laughed and rolled over to use the stones of the patio to scratch his back. When he was done, he shook his fur, and then once again sat down and looked at me sideways.

"Good job using Koog's eyebrow, Kid!"

"Thanks."

"Raffle, I know your birthday is coming up soon, and you are anxious to be promoted then."

"Does it show?"

Heg laughed.

"That bad, huh?"

"It's not bad to want to take on more responsibility in serving Kax. Just remember that is what we are doing: Kax's will."

"But, how do we know what Kax's will is?"

"By praying to Kax. That is how to know Kax's will so we can serve Kax, and not ourselves."

"But Kax never answers me at all."

"You're wrong there. Kax always answers prayer, but often we don't get the answer that we want or expect."

"I never get any answer at all!"

Heg raised one eyebrow.

"I don't!"

"Think back on all your conversations with Kax, and remember what has happened afterward. I am certain you will find that all your prayers have been answered in one of three ways:

One: Yes! Here is my help.

Two: The time for this has not yet come.

Three: I have something better in mind."

CHERISE KELLEY

CHAPTER 17: LURING

Luring prey animals proved to be immensely fun! It was a good thing I practiced someplace away from home, though. What's that you say? What could go wrong, leading a bunch of harmless prey animals? Have you heard of the Pied Piper of Hamelin? Well, no, that's a bad example. Let's just say if you lead, make sure you know where you're going!

My mistress' mother keeps horses, and one day we all went to visit the stables. This was west a bit, near the wealthy desert oasis community of Palm Springs. The stable owners have twenty acres there with a large barn, patio clubhouse, riding trails, and a show arena. They rent out barn stalls, and this is where my mistress' mother boards her horses. All the boarders visit their horses on the weekends, and there is a party atmosphere. Everyone greeted us when we arrived.

"Hello!"

"Great to see you!"

"Glad you could come!"

"It's barbeque lunch today!"

It wasn't your typical barbeque, though. This is Southern California. People dress to impress at all times here. These people were dressed up in

"English riding clothes" that smelled new and that must have been expensive, given how they admired each other's garments.

"Ooh! Are those this season's Ariats?"

"Ah! Love your new Arista riding vest!"

"Oh! Cavallos come in caffe color!"

Wonder of wonders, I was the only "dog" there that day. I got petted, commented on, and pampered until my head swelled too big for my body. I was also sneakingly given so many table scraps I walked around with a bloated stomach and had to puke twice. Don't worry. I do have manners. I puked in the bushes when no one was looking, far away from the patio clubhouse.

The stable did have a few cats. They were smart enough to notice that all the humans loved me, so they left me alone. It was a bit disconcerting to hear them hissing at me from under cars all day, but nothing I wasn't used to from the early days at my new den, before Puritan got herself locked up in the bathroom. As with her, sure enough, their minds were all purple with thoughts of the hunt, and impenetrable to me because of these thoughts.

The best thing about the stables was all the chickens. Yes, I said chickens! They were pet chickens, just there for atmosphere, I guess. They ate the stray seeds from the straw that lined all the horse stalls. Chickens came up to greet each new car that arrived. They stood still to be petted by the humans! They made the funniest squawking noises whenever I lunged at them. I suppose the cats knew better than to mess with the chickens and anger the humans who fed the cats. There were dozens of chickens and a few roosters. They were spread out all over the place, but mostly near the barn and the clubhouse patio, where people who were eating outside often tossed them strips of hamburger bun. Every time a human turned around, he about tripped over a chicken.

I found a great opportunity to test my skill at playing mental movies in the minds of prey animals, to see if I could lure them to do my bidding. It might have gone better if I hadn't been on a leash, obligated to go wherever my master went.

There was this plate of food that one of the humans had abandoned, on an outside table. I smelled the barbequed hamburger and potato salad on that plate, and I wanted it, even though my stomach was about full enough to burst. Here was the perfect task for my little chicken army!

I composed the mental movie. I imagined all the chickens going to that plate of food, taking a piece of food in their beaks, bringing it to me, and leaving it at my feet for me to eat! I was sitting under another table nearby, next to my humans. I played the mental movie over a few times in my own head, just to make sure nothing awful happened. It looked great!

In my mind's eye, I searched out the dozens of chicken and rooster minds spread out all around me. Chicken minds are kind of boring. Not one of them was angry, excited, happy, or even frustrated about anything. I didn't even sense any fear, which is the emotion most associated with, you know, being chicken. It probably helped that these were pet chickens on a ranch where no one ate their eggs and the cats weren't allowed to mess with them and the fences kept the coyotes out. Yeah, probably that helped.

I couldn't believe how easy it was to play the

mental movie for all the chickens. As soon as I found their minds, I played it. Simple as that.

Immediately, all the chickens in the area swooped down on that abandoned food and started pecking at it. The first few arrived at my feet and dropped their little pieces of hamburger, or bun, or potato. So far, so good! I licked up the scraps of food and waited for them to move on so that the others could drop their beak-fulls of bounty.

Only, they didn't move on. That was where the mental movie ended, so they were free to go on about their business, only they didn't have any business. They stayed right where they were.

Other chickens started to peck on the front chickens' backs with their beak-fulls of food, telling them to move away so that they could get to me with the food they had so kindly brought over for me. They all started that funny squawking noise, and more and more of them kept coming. Feathers started to fly.

Humans were starting to notice, and to tap each other on the shoulder and point out the spectacle of a dozen chickens all fighting to get close to a dog!

"Why do they all want to be near that dog?"

"I don't know, Billie. Eat your meat."

"Look at all those chickens!"

"Yeah, woo! Pass the salt."

Meanwhile, someone had picked up the emptying plate of food and tossed it in the garbage. This did not dissuade the many chickens which were still arriving. Oh no! Rather, the chickens jumped into the garbage can and dug for the plate of food.

"Wow, I'm pretty persuasive with the chicken

population," I was thinking. "This could come in handy!" I puffed out my chest almost as big as Lido had when he told me of his success with Skil. I was a big shot chicken herder. Yes, I was. I wondered if I could get any special recognition for that. Was there someone I could notify?

And then my master, who had me on a leash, said something I had not foreseen when I composed my movie.

"Where's the men's room?"

"Over there by ice cream stand."

"In that corner, up against the fence?"

"Yeah. Want me to hold Raffle's leash?"

"Nah, I'll take him with me."

Of course, the chickens followed us over toward the ice cream stand, trying all the time to drop the food at my feet. I had to keep up with my master, though, and he was walking with purpose, if you know what I mean. He opened the door of the men's room and pulled me in there with him. He walked right past the urinal and into a stall, where he did some business for several minutes.

I could hear pandemonium outside the men's room door. Half of it was all the chickens squawking as they piled up on top of each other and tried to get through the door. The other half was the havoc the chickens wreaked as distracted humans walked away with ice cream cones in their hands.

Splat! Splat! Ice cream hit the cement patio as unsuspecting patrons tripped over chickens.

"Louisa! You've spilled ice cream on your nice new jacket!"

"What the?"

"Eeeeeeaaaaaaak!"

"Someone do something about all these chickens!"

Yeah, someone do something about these chickens. Of course, that someone was me! I quickly composed and sent all the chickens and roosters a mental movie of them all stepping away from the building.

Instantly, the chicken squawking stopped. I had a new appreciation for just how easy some of us Kaxians would find it to herd animals. I had the distinct impression that even the huge cows my mom tells me her side of the family herds over in Australia would be no problem, with my mental movies.

The humans continued to make distressed noises for a few more minutes, but finally those, too, died down.

Human hearing leaves much to the human imagination, I guess. My master hadn't even noticed that anything unusual was going on, but his mate and her mother filled him in once we rejoined them at our table.

"Scott! You missed it!"

"What?"

"The chickens all went crazy over something by the men's room door!"

"Yeah! They were squabbling like mad!"

"People started tripping over them."

"And everyone was spilling ice cream..."

"You really missed quite a show!"

Like I said, I was really glad I had practiced this here at the stables, where they thought it was quite a show, and something to laugh about. It was a good thing I hadn't tried this at home, but I planned to do that next.

***

My Nique neighbors still ran out through their doggie door just to taunt me, whenever my humans let me out back through the sliding glass door, to do my business.

"Did your mommie let you come out?"

"Be careful, now."

"Don't hurt yourself."

"Cry if you can't find the tree, Punkie."

I was more determined than ever to get even with them, and now I had a new weapon in my arsenal: I would sic my prey animals on those two pesky Niques.

From my chicken experience, I knew I had to include a critter's exit strategy, when I sent it a mental movie. Amusing as the chicken pile-up at the ice cream stand had been, it had also been too much of a spectacle. Sooner rather than later, a spectacle like that would violate our prime command from Kax (and from Nique, but who cares about that?):

No humans can know that dogs are aliens.

So, when I turned my attention to luring prey animals for my selfish purpose of wreaking revenge against my two pesky Nique neighbors, I kept the prey animals' exit strategies in mind.

"What's the worst thing I can do to a couple of Niques without actually harming them?" I was thinking to myself. "I know! I'll mess with their food!" Guys hate it when you mess with their food.

I could smell their two small bowls full of dry dog food inside their house, just past their doggie door. Their humans kept their bowls always full of food, and let the Niques eat as much as they wanted.

"Heh!" I thought, "If the Niques can go in and out the doggie door, so could other vermin."

Reaching out with my mind's eye, I located some very small minds, inside the walls of the Niques' house. They were spread far apart and traveling alarmingly quickly all over the house. I guessed they were searching for food. These minds were not as bored as the chickens' minds had been. They were not pets, not pampered nor protected. Yet, they were not being hunted, merely scavenging. They were receptive. I was starting to be able to tell. I wasn't sure how I knew, but I did know my mental movies would work on these mice.

I composed the mental movie, reminding myself to get them back to their normal activities once they had done my errand. In the movie, they came to the small dishes full of food and took all they wanted, and then went back into the walls and scurried around in there until they got tired, and then they went to sleep. I hoped that was enough to get them back to doing what they normally did autonomously, but I reminded myself to check on the poor little mice later, just in case. And then, I played my mental movie in their little mouse minds.

It worked! The mice ate up the Niques' food that was in their food bowls.

At first, the Niques' humans just refilled the food bowls and didn't think anything of it. I knew when the humans started to notice the food was disappearing because I could hear them talking about it, clear over there in the house next door.

"Did you feed the dogs this morning?"
"Yeah, I did."
"Well, they don't have any food."

"No way!"

The Niques themselves noticed their food was disappearing, of course, but so long as their humans kept replacing the food, its disappearance wasn't bothering the Niques any. It took a week for the humans to become concerned that their dogs' food kept disappearing so quickly.

"Why in the world am I filling the dogs' food bowls so often?"

"I've been filling them, too!"

"Where can all this food be going?"

I had to keep playing my mental movie for the mice, to make them keep taking the food. I did this at strategic times, so that the humans didn't notice. However, the humans were now putting food in the dishes eight times a day. The mice had trouble eating so much. I could smell the mouse puke all the way over in my house. I didn't want the humans to start smelling it.

I had to bring in more mice.

Finally, I ended up bringing in ants, too. I started a whole colony of ants under the house next door.

About the time the humans next door started getting angry about how the Niques' food was disappearing so quickly, they couldn't help but notice the ants. The infestation was so bad, I kinda sorta heard them shrieking about ants coming out of the shower head. The landlord called an exterminator who came for the ant problem, and he killed off all the mice, while he was at it.

The Niques were supposed to suffer, but the only ones suffering next door were the poor mice I had used for my selfish revenge scheme. And the humans.

"Well, that didn't work out quite the way I wanted it to." I just thought this in my head. I wasn't frustrated enough to be talking to myself out loud or anything. Not me!

***

Next, I tried birds. There were lots of pigeons around who I guessed were the pigeons that the former tenants used for their drug smuggling operations. Carrier pigeons. They roosted under the eaves of our house, now that their coops were gone. I didn't have any messages to send, but I thought that was a cool idea I might use some day, if I needed to communicate with my master and he was far away without me.

The next time I was outside doing my business, sure enough, my two pesky Nique neighbors charged out through their doggie door to pester me.

"Ooh! The little momma's boy got out!"

"Can you find the tree by yourself, Punkie?"

Well, the joke was on them, because from all sides they were pelted with pigeon poop! I had all the pigeons drop whatever they had on the noisy Niques, and then return to their roosts.

"Haha! I probably shouldn't laugh at your misfortune, but hahaha! it's so funny!"

I just stood there laughing at them. It felt great!

***

Squirrels worked great, too. I got them to pelt the little Niques with pine cones from the trees in their back yard. It got so they were afraid to go out through their little doggie door! I won!

CHAPTER 18: VACATION

One day, my humans started talking about going on a vacation. The memories told me this meant going far from home, but only for a week or two.

"I want to take Raffle on a camping trip."

My master was talking to his mate.

"Ooh! That sounds fun!"

"Here is a book that describes various camp grounds three or four hours' drive from here. Let's pick one out and plan our trip."

"OK."

Going away from the den is much more complicated for humans than it is for Kaxians or wolves (or Niques, but who cares about them?). My humans called both their employers and arranged for the time off. They called the landlord and arranged to have the grass cut and the fall leaves raked. However, soon it was settled that we would be going away for two weeks.

I would be turning one year old in the middle of our vacation time, and that meant I would be an adult Kaxian, no longer a non-qualified puppy. After that, I would be eligible for promotion, at least age-wise.

The wolf in me loved the trip, including the

155

drive. My humans didn't use the air conditioner, so the truck cab windows were open wide. From my place behind the seats, I could just manage to stick my nose out the passenger door window.

Wow! There were a thousand different scents flowing past my nose each second. In addition to all the scents of the highway: rubber tires, exhaust, hot metal, asphalt... I smelled grasses, trees, bushes, animals, birds, and even insects. Each scent brought its source to my mind for contemplation for a split second, and then it was on to the next scent. The experience was intoxicating. I was perfectly content to just sit there with my nose out the window, smelling this world go by.

The wolf in me loved our campground, too. Summer had gone by, and the cooler days of fall had come, so we had the place almost all to ourselves. Only three of the forty campsites were inhabited. Our site was fairly large, a quarter acre or so, and all we had on it was our little pickup truck and a large tent. The site had its own fire ring and picnic table. There were hills and large pines and live-oak trees all around, so we had privacy. We could not see any of the human inhabitants of the other campsites, although of course I could hear them and smell them.

There was food to be hunted everywhere:
birds,
rabbits,
squirrels,
snakes,
raccoons,
possums...

But, my master and mistress ate stuff out of cans. Humans are weird. I wasn't complaining, though. No way. They let me lick the food off their dishes before they used the suds! I had to admit that canned chili and baked beans tasted good out here.

There was a lake near our campsite, and they let me off the leash to swim. It was the first time I swam, this life. Swimming is something everyone should do every chance they get! It's so much fun, and feels so good, and is so good for you.

Fishing was the most fun activity for my master, and they did eat what he caught. Once I figured out what he was trying to do when he took out that stick with the string on it and threw it out into the water, I sent the fish mental movies in which they bit the worms he stuck on a hook at the end of the string. He started bringing in one fish after another, and his mind turned the brightest pink I ever saw, with excitement. It made me happy to make him so happy, and we enjoyed our days together immensely.

My master was weird about the fish, though. He easily caught fifty fish a day for two weeks, but for some reason, he only wanted to keep ten of them. Ten fish was all he wanted to show for two weeks of hunting fish! Isn't that weird?

He put the first ten fish he caught in a plastic cage that he set in the shallow part of the lake. Whenever he caught a bigger fish, he put it in the cage and threw a smaller fish back into the lake. My humans took the biggest ten fish home in an iced cooler, and they did eat them. I was proud of my human fish hunter.

We did have a lot of fun on the camping trip to the woods. Each evening, my humans would build a fire to heat canned food and roast marshmallows.

Sometimes my mistress would sing. They took me on walks around the lake and up into the nearby hills. We explored the land all around the campground.

The wolf in me was having a good old time. He loved this "back to nature" stuff. However, I am only a tiny bit wolf.

Most of me is Kaxian, and I was out of earshot, nose range, and suggestion range of every Kaxian I knew (and every Nique, too, but who cares about them?). The tiny bit of me that is wolf was having a grand old time. The Kaxian me was near panic almost every moment.

I couldn't help but remember the last time I had been so far from everyone. In my head, I knew my new humans would never abandon me. I knew they loved me. However, the heart is cruel. No matter how many times my head told me I had nothing to worry about, my heart kept fearing my beloved humans had brought me here to abandon me.

My fear of abandonment was especially bad at meal time. I simply could not get myself to eat unless I could see that my humans were settled down and not about to leave me. I always ate with my ears tuned to their activity. If they got up while I was eating, then I stopped eating and turned to follow them, wherever they were going. They found this annoying when emptying their bladders!

Heg was right, though. My parents had trained me correctly. I knew what I had to do.

"Kax! Thank you for giving me these two loving and attentive humans. Please help me not be so afraid they'll abandon me. I know I seem ungrateful, in my fear."

I didn't expect an answer.

Imagine my surprise when one came!

I didn't so much hear a voice in my head as see moving pictures, a little like Heg's power and a lot like my power of suggestion at work—and, I now realized, like the memories. This was just like my Kaxian memories that came back to me gradually as I grew up, the way Mom and Dad had told me they would.

Only, the mental movie I saw now was of much larger scope than the pictures Heg showed me or than the mental movies I had shown Randy, my master, Mister's master, the rest of my old Kaxian pack, or any of the prey animals. Somehow, every Kaxian—both on Earth and back on our planet—was in this mental movie. Most importantly, it showed me the very nature of Kax. It showed me that some Kaxians, like me, are meant to hear Kax and to pass on to the others the will of Kax.

Now I knew what I had been training for!

And then the mental movie got even more amazing. It showed me what had been hidden from my puppy self.

This duty of being one of the Earthly voices of Kax was what I had done in every life, and what I would continue to do in all my lives to come. Now, on my birthday, when I was once again an adult, all the memories came back to me. I was myself once again, truly reborn to my Kaxian destiny.

***

I greatly enjoyed the rest of the vacation after that! My puppy self still feared being abandoned, but now the puppy part of me was as tiny as the wolf part, and I had memories from 98 lives to draw on.

***

"Come on, Raffle! Let's go to Pet Smart and meet your new baby brother!"

It was a few months after we went on my birthday vacation when my master came home by himself, leaving my mistress at the store while he very considerately came to get me and take me to meet their new dog before they brought him home. I found out later how they had managed to pick out a new "brother" for me without my having a chance to screen him first.

They'd gone to the store to get things for me, and to look around. They hadn't brought me because the trip hadn't even been planned. They'd stopped at the store on their way home from the movies.

When my humans entered the store, they noticed that the humane society had ambushed them by bringing in a bunch of animals that were up for adoption. There were about 50 kennels set up near the entrance inside the store, with big signs saying "Adopt Me!" Not even a human could have missed the display.

At first, my humans ignored the animals and went about shopping around for toys and treats for me, as they did every week or so, bless them. They went up and down every aisle in the big-dog section, handling squeaky toys, raw-hides, and even cookies meant for dogs. They never bought any of those silly dog cookies.

Gradually, my humans' curiosity about what types of animals the humane society had brought to be adopted got the better of them.

"Wanna go check out the animals they brought for adoption from the pound?"

"I thought you'd never ask!"

They went over and started looking in the kennels. There were a few cats, but the vast majority of the kennels contained abandoned Kaxians.

"We really should get Raffle a girlfriend, to keep him company when one of us can't be with him."

"Or a buddy, anyway."

"Well, yeah, a buddy would be good."

"Look! This female kind of looks like him."

"Yeah, she kind of does."

"Excuse me, Sir?"

"Yes?"

"Can we see this dog outside her kennel?"

"Sure."

They petted her and tried to play with her, but she was skittish and timid. She barely raised her head up to look them in the eyes. Still, my mistress was hung up on the idea of getting me a girlfriend. She tried really hard to like this skittish, timid dog that looked like me.

My master had another Kaxian in mind to be my buddy, though.

"Let's put her back. Sir! Yeah, we're not interested in this one after all. Thanks."

He showed her the dog he had in mind. It was funny: somehow, they had decided to adopt a dog during the hour they'd been in the store, and now it was just a question of which dog they were going to adopt!

The dog my master had in mind for my buddy, and the one my mistress determined would be my new "baby brother," is a show-bred English springer spaniel with more wolf in him than I have. He's all black except for white smatterings on his paws, chin, throat, stomach, and the tip of his tail.

"This one looks like he'll play more than that other one."

"Yeah, maybe she is old."

"This one is a puppy, so he'll play a lot!"

"He's a puppy? He's so big, though."

"Yeah, see? Look at his teeth."

The pound employee pulled the springer spaniel's lips back so that my humans could see that he lacked teeth in the sides of his mouth.

"Well, I guess Raffle will be helping us raise this puppy!"

"Can you hold him while we go get him a collar and a leash?"

"Of course. There is some paperwork you need to fill out first, though."

"OK."

"He has been named Oreo already by us pound employees. You can change the name, of course, but he does respond to it."

"Hm."

"We'll have to think about that. Thanks."

They filled out the paperwork, made it official, and were halfway through picking out not only a collar and leash but a sleeping kennel, dog dishes, and more toys before they started wondering what my reaction might be to them bringing a strange dog into our home.

"What about Raffle? Won't he try to eat Oreo, if we bring him into the house?"

"Oh yeah. Hm. Maybe it would be better if we brought Raffle here to meet Oreo."

"Yeah, Raffle is less territorial and more friendly when he meets other dogs away from home."

They bought all the new stuff along with the collar and leash, took it over to the humane society's display, picked up Oreo, and put his new leash and collar on him.

"We need for our current dog to meet Oreo before we will be sure we can take him home. My husband is going to get Raffle and bring him here to meet Oreo. I'm pretty sure it will be OK, but we need to do this just in case."

"Yeah, OK, we understand."

So this is where we came in. My mistress was sitting in the store with Oreo and a shopping cart full of stuff for him. I was in the truck with my master, on my way to meet my new "baby brother."

And that was the first time Oreo ran away. He slipped out of his collar and ran under some displays to escape down the main aisle, toward the reptile aquariums in the back of the store. My mistress had a shopping cart full of stuff she didn't want to get stolen, so she wheeled it with her as she chased him. She finally had to leave it in the aisle and follow him into a display of kennels before she caught the little stinker.

The two of them had returned to the front of the store and were seated by the humane society's display when I first saw Oreo.

"You're no puppy!"

"Aw, relax. If your human wants to treat me like a puppy, then I'm all for it."

She did want to treat Oreo like a puppy. She seemed concerned about us barking at each other, too.

"Be nice, Raffle!"

"Haha! You have to be nice to me now!"

163

"Be nice, Oreo!"

He wasn't going to cooperate, but I quickly composed and sent him a mental movie of the two of us paling around together: barking at the Niques together through our back yard fence, for one thing. Our mistress was happy that we had stopped barking at each other, and she petted both of us, one with each hand.

One of the pound employees came up to our humans just as we were leaving Pet Smart. The pound employee spoke in a whisper, as if that could keep Oreo or I from hearing him. Silly human.

"What's the kennel for?"

"We crate train. It's for Oreo to sleep in."

"Oh. Well, you may find him more resistant to crate training than most puppies his age."

"Why's that?"

The pound employee was still whispering.

"He was abandoned in a crate."

My mistress started crying as she cuddled Oreo and pet him and tried to reassure him he would not be abandoned again.

"Oh my poor, poor puppy. We're going to love you and take care of you and never abandon you. I promise."

My master joined in on petting Oreo, and agreed to the promises his mate made.

"Yes, yes, Boy, yes."
***

Our humans loaded Oreo's sleeping crate, dishes, and toys into the camper shell of our truck, and then they seat-belted me behind the passenger seat and Oreo behind the driver seat. On the way home, they parked in a parking lot at a restaurant, took us both out for a short walk to do our business, and then seat-belted us behind the seats in the truck again. They went inside the restaurant. It was winter now, so the windows were only cracked open, not wide open like in summer.

"Oh, forget this. I'm getting out of here!"

Oreo started chewing through the seat-belt that tied him to the truck through his car harness.

"Quit doing that!"

Oreo laughed.

"Just because she thinks I'm a puppy and she told you to be nice to me, that doesn't mean I gotta do what you say."

I tried playing a mental movie of him going to sleep, but Oreo's mind was bright lavender with resentment, aimed at me, no doubt.

"It's pointless, though! Even if you chew all the way through the seat-belt, you're still locked inside this truck cab!"

But Oreo didn't listen. He kept chewing on the seat-belt. He was almost all the way through it when our humans came back.

"Ahhhhh!"

"What's wrong?"

This was the calm but resigned voice of our mistress.

"Oreo chewed the seat-belt all up!"

"Oh no!"

My master's mind was a red ball of rage. I hate to think what might have become of my new "baby brother" if the seat hadn't been between him and my master, but to give him credit, my master stormed off into the desert to cool off. My mistress wisely let her mate go off alone to calm his rage. When he got back to the truck, I fully expected my master to declare we were taking Oreo right back to the pound.

I debated playing my master a mental movie to stop that from happening. His mind was a calm blue once more, and after all, Oreo was a fellow Kaxian. But, he was so obnoxious! I didn't need to decide, though. My master aimed the truck toward home. My mistress sighed, and we all kept quiet the rest of the way home, each lost in his or her own thoughts.

We got home a little while later. It was dark out, and time for me to be fed. Time for Oreo to be fed, too, I guessed. Before unbuckling the ruined seat-belt and letting Oreo out of the truck, our master petted him while he gave him a little lecture. I backed the lecture up with a mental movie.

"Oreo, Puppy, you can't chew seat-belts. No! Now, you aren't going to ride in the car again until we have a muzzle for you, and for the rest of your life, you are going to wear a muzzle whenever you are in the car."

It turned out Oreo was a pet-me, like Skil. As soon as our human started petting him, he rolled over onto his back and exposed his belly to be scratched. Our human obliged gently and with love.

Our mistress stood back smiling, watching her mate pet her new "puppy." She spoke with excitement.

"Shall we take him inside and feed them both and then show Oreo around his new home?"

My master's voice was soothing.

"Yeah, Puppy. Come inside and see your new home."

My mistress took us both through the gate

into the back yard to do more business on our way into the house while my master carried Oreo's sleeping kennel, dishes, and toys inside. Our Nique neighbors came out to chide us, of course. Also of course, they had heard our human lecturing Oreo, and they could smell Oreo's true age for this life, just as I could.

"Haha!"

"How's it going, three-year-old 'puppy'?"

"I'm glad I don't get muzzled in the car."

For once, I agreed with our Nique neighbors, so this time I didn't tell the squirrels to pummel them with pine cones. Oreo took it in stride, though. I was beginning to think he had no shame.

"It's going great! I've got two pushover humans to feed me and pet me, and Raffle here has to be nice to me because they said so. Life is good!"

"Well, good luck with the puppy stuff."

"Yeah, your humans have to let you out."

"You don't have a doggie door like we do."

"Haha!"

The Niques tried to rile Oreo up, but his mind stayed cool as a cucumber. In spite of all the annoyance I still harbored for my new "baby brother" because of his lack of respect for our humans, I was impressed at how he avoided being annoyed by the Niques.

"Whatever, Dudes."

Just then, our mistress called us in for food, and we took off running for it. Food is good!

After we ate, our humans showed Oreo around the house. They showed him our sleeping den with their bed and our two sleeping kennels first.

"Go in your house, Raffle."

I went inside my sleeping kennel. It's really much more like a wolf den than the big bedroom. I kind of like it in there. It's my refuge.

Oreo did not want to go inside his sleeping kennel. We all understood why, but my master was determined.

"Go in your house, Oreo."

Oreo wasn't budging. My master picked him up and put him in his kennel.

"Good boy, Oreo."

As soon as my master let Oreo go, he flew out of the sleeping kennel and started threatening to run away. Of course, I was the only one who could understand what he was saying.

"That's enough of this kennel stuff, and I'm not wearing a muzzle, either. First chance I get, I'm out of here for good."

And then my mistress complicated my world almost beyond belief by making me Oreo's caretaker while she was busy earning money to buy our food and her mate was sleeping so he could do the same.

"Come, Raffle. Look, see how I am cleaning Oreo's face? See? He has crumbs on his cheeks and eye-snot coming out of his eyes. We need to clean his face for him. Let's clean his ears, too."

She showed me how to clean the "puppy's" ears, and then went on.

"Raffle, Oreo is just a puppy, and we need to take care of him. You will have to care for him while I am busy with my work."

She petted me then, and smiled at me as she sealed my fate by idly giving me a binding command.

"Take care of your brother, Raffle. Keep him from running away from me again."

CHERISE KELLEY

THANK YOU

Thank you for reading this book!

Please sign up for my mailing list so that I can tell you when the next Dog Aliens book is released.

http://eepurl.com/oQOgn

I only send messages to my mailing list when I release new books. I do not share any part of the list with anyone.

AUTHOR'S NOTE

This is partly the true story of how we adopted our dog and named him. Sometimes, I think the rest of the story is true, too. Raffle is such an intelligent and obedient dog. I have never encountered another dog who was so eager to please his humans.

However, I admit that he is the first Australian Cow Dog I ever met, let alone the first Queensland Heeler. Perhaps they are an exceptional breed.

If you would like to see real life photos of Raffle, then please visit my blog:

http://size12bystpatricksday.blogspot.com/

Thank you again,
Cherise Kelley